THE CHERRY VALLEY MIDDLE SCHOOL

DEAR KNOW-IT-ALL

WITHDRAWN

★ ★ ★

Stop the Presses!

by RACHEL WISE

Simon Spotlight
New York   London   Toronto   Sydney   New Delhi

This book is a work of fiction. Any references to historical events, real people, or real places are used fictitiously. Other names, characters, places, and events are products of the author's imagination, and any resemblance to actual events or places or persons, living or dead, is entirely coincidental.

SIMON SPOTLIGHT

An imprint of Simon & Schuster Children's Publishing Division
1230 Avenue of the Americas, New York, New York 10020
First Simon Spotlight edition July 2014
Copyright © 2014 by Simon & Schuster, Inc. All rights reserved, including the right of reproduction in whole or in part in any form.
SIMON SPOTLIGHT and colophon are registered trademarks of Simon & Schuster, Inc.
Text by Sheila Sweeny Higginson

For information about special discounts for bulk purchases, please contact Simon & Schuster Special Sales at 1-866-506-1949 or business@simonandschuster.com.
Manufactured in the United States of America 0514 OFF
10 9 8 7 6 5 4 3 2 1
ISBN 978-1-4424-9798-6 (hc)
ISBN 978-1-4424-9797-9 (pbk)
ISBN 978-1-4424-9799-3 (eBook)
Library of Congress Catalog Card Number 2014936483

Chapter 1

SPRING BREAK FAILS TO GARNER EXCITEMENT AT MARTONE HOUSEHOLD

★ ★ ★

Have you ever gotten up close and personal with a piece of paper? Like when you're writing a report for school, or working on some problems in your math book, do you stop for a moment and hold the page up to the light, examining it in all its glorious papery beauty? Sometimes you can see tiny bits of pulp or fibers and it's really pretty. Or sometimes the paper shines so much that the words look like they're vibrating on the page. Sometimes it's so thin that you can almost see right through it and it's almost like a magic trick that there are words on the page. I love the way it smells, too—

sometimes new, like when you crack open a notebook for the first time in the fall; and sometimes it smells musty, like it's been sitting in a supply closet all summer.

Okay, okay, I'm sorry for rambling. I know what you're probably thinking. And I promise that I have not lost my mind because of the insomnia I've been having. I've been following my new sleep hygiene plan pretty closely, and it's working. Well, maybe not so closely on the nights when my best friend, Hailey Jones, sleeps over, but definitely during the school week. It's been lights out and eyes closed until my alarm clock (turned away from me so the light doesn't shine in my face) goes off.

But let's get back to paper. I've always loved to write—and read—but it wasn't until my date—er, field trip—to see our newspaper's print run with Michael Lawrence that I began to fully appreciate the unique beauty of the printed page. We took a tour of FlyPrint, the company that prints the *Cherry Valley Voice*, and Mr. Dunleavy, our sales rep, showed us the enormous rolls of paper, the printing plates, and the presses in action. It was, like, the coolest thing ever. I mean, I love the rush of writing a story for the paper on a deadline, but actually seeing the story being printed? Totally cool. Even better, I witnessed it all side by side with my writing partner and future fantastic boyfriend. It was truly a magical moment.

Since the trip, though, I've been looking around and noticing that not a lot of my friends seem to feel the same way I do about the whole paper experience. It seems like everyone's always wrapped up in some electronic device. Take my sister, Allie, for instance. Sometimes I'll be sitting in my room when I hear my phone chime and see that there's a text message from her. *That's odd*, I think. *Allie was home five minutes ago. Did she leave the house in spy mode? I didn't even hear her go.* And you know what? It always turns out that she never even left the house. She is texting me from her bedroom, which is *right next to my bedroom*. Would it really be so difficult for her to walk across the hall and talk to me in person? Do you find me that repulsive, Big Sister, that you can't even look at me?

Allie isn't alone, though. I was reading a study (and I admit, I was reading it on my computer), and it said that 63 percent of teenagers use text messages to communicate with their friends every day. Meanwhile, only 35 percent said that they talk face-to-face with their friends outside of school on a daily basis. That seems like a pretty sad statistic to me. I mean, I love, love talking to Hailey. I can't imagine just texting or e-mailing her. Mrs. Osborne, our school librarian, says that as long as we're reading, it doesn't matter if it's on a screen or a printed page, but I still feel a little sad when I see a big pile of yesterday's unsold daily newspapers sitting outside the door of the local store, waiting to be picked up. There's even a Website devoted to chronicling the death of metropolitan dailies, which is what they call the daily newspapers. It's called "Newspaper Death Watch." How tragic is that?

You want to know what's even more tragic? I haven't heard from Michael Lawrence in five whole days. Not a face-to-face conversation, not a phone call, not even a "Hey, what's up, Pasty?" text. I'm starting to have Crush Withdrawal Syndrome. I mean, I'm not sure I remember the exact shade of blue that his incredibly blue eyes truly are because I have not been able to stare deeply into them. It's reaching crisis level, for sure.

I was kind of in a grouchy mood, since on top of my not seeing Michael, my mom suggested that Allie and I clean out our bedrooms. Allie and I don't have much in common except we both are kind of pack rats. I like to keep books, newspapers, and magazines. Allie likes to keep every bit of clothing she's ever worn. And she remembers them, too. If I borrow something she hasn't worn in three years without asking her, the minute she sees it on me she'll say something like, "What are you doing wearing that sweater? I bought it to wear to Kim's birthday party (in 2010!). I love that sweater." It's crazy. Anyway, Mom said a thorough cleaning out of both our rooms was long overdue. I'm not a happy camper. I like my room the way it is and I hate change. So you can see the problem.

I heard my mom rustling around in her room,

so I decided to go and see what she was doing and maybe torture her a little by whining about how bored I was. But instead of finding her buried in a pile of receipts and bank statements, I caught her looking in a big, flowery hatbox.

"What are you doing, Mom?" I asked. "Looking for an old tax form?"

Mom jumped when she heard my voice, obviously not expecting either Allie or me to barge in on her.

"Oh no." She chuckled nervously. "It's just some old stuff. I thought that since I've been making you girls clean out your rooms, I should take a break from the numbers crunching and clean out some things too."

"Can I see what's in it?" I asked.

"Sure," Mom said. "I'll probably throw most of it out anyway. I don't know why I've been keeping it up there. It's just taking up space."

Mom and I plopped on the bed and started taking things out of the box. There were some reasonably interesting items in there, like a hospital bracelet from the time Mom had her appendix removed and a dried corsage from her high school prom. But to me, the most fascinating thing was a stack of papers—of course!—tied up in a red ribbon. The paper itself wasn't so special; it looked mostly like loose-leaf that had been crumpled up and had turned slightly yellow with age. There may have even been some splashes of sauce on a few of the pages. I could tell from the ribbon that even though they looked pretty ordinary, this pile was not a collection of Mom's middle school reports.

"What are these?" I asked as I held up the pile.

"Oh, you can put those in the recycling bin," Mom said. "They're just some letters from a boy I used to be friends with in eighth grade."

Friends. That's a good one, Mom. That's what I always say about Michael Lawrence. We've been friends since kindergarten.

"So you don't mind if I read them, then?" I asked.

I had Mom cornered. If she said no, she was admitting that they were special and private.

"Um, sure, if you want," Mom answered. "You're just going to think they're boring and silly."

I almost laughed out loud when I read the first one. It was sooooo middle school.

Dear Nina,

I'm glad that we're friends. I'd really like to be more than friends. Do you feel the same way? If you do, check yes. If not, check no. Don't worry. We'll still be friends either way.

Yes ☑

No ☐

-John

"MOM!" I screamed. "Why didn't you ever give this to him?"

Mom's cheeks actually started to turn red. She was blushing about a boy she'd known eons ago!

"I thought I would just tell him how I felt," she replied.

"And how did that go?" I wondered, thinking I knew the answer: not well.

"Pretty well," she said, and I looked up. "We were kind of a thing until the middle of high school."

"Kind of a thing?" I laughed. "What kind of a thing is that?" It was weird talking to Mom about boys she dated, like, when she was my age.

"A boyfriend/girlfriend kind of thing," Mom said.

"Are you kidding?" I yelled. "My mother had a boyfriend in eighth grade and I don't? *I am hopeless!*"

"Sam, please," Mom said, still blushing a little. "He wasn't really my boyfriend then. He just had a crush on me . . . and I had a little crush on him, too. You know, kind of like you and that Michael Lawrence boy."

I decided to ignore her. I didn't want to talk about Michael Lawrence just then. And besides, I don't think Michael and I are just a thing. I mean, he's the love of my life.

I started flipping through the letters. The first

few weren't very interesting, just regular stuff like "Meet me at the library today," or "Do you have time to study for the English test?" But then I thought about the pictures of Mom I had seen from that time and I thought about myself and sighed. We weren't that different, me and that girl Mom used to be. If Michael handed me a note saying, "Meet me at the library today," my heart would be doing little leaps of joy. And I would probably try to save the letter.

I started digging deeper into the pile, and the letters got juicier. I gasped when I read this one:

Dear Nina,

I feel like the whole world disappears when I'm with you. I don't have anything to worry about. It's just you and your beautiful smile, and nothing else matters. You make me really happy, and I had an awesome time just talking to you last night. I feel like I could sit and talk with you for hours and hours.

—John

Now, that kind of writing could cause some heart palpitations! I sighed and leaned back on Mom's pillow. I couldn't even imagine how I would feel if Michael wrote me a note like that. Blown away, I guess.

"Mom, was John your first love?" I asked.

"I guess you could say that," Mom answered.

"So why haven't I ever heard anything about him before?" I asked. "And what happened to him anyway?"

"Oh, we just, um, we just kind of grew apart," Mom said.

Mom isn't usually the stammering type, so I knew I would have to use my reporter's instinct and dig deeper.

"Why did you grow apart?" I asked. "Did he move? Did you go to different high schools? Did your parents forbid you to see each other?"

"No, Sam. We went to the same high school," replied Mom. "That was part of the problem. . . . There was someone else there. . . ."

"Oh, I'm really sorry, Mom. Did he drop you for another girl?" I asked, wanting to kick myself for prying and bringing up painful memories. "What a jerk!"

Or maybe not so painful—Mom was laughing.

"Hardly," she said. "There was another boy that I liked, and well, it kind of got complicated."

I was shocked. Who knew Mom had such a complicated love life when she was young? I'd always figured she was just some mathlete who was too busy doing equations to even notice boys.

"It was a fun time, Sam," Mom said. "I hope you enjoy your teen years as much as I did."

"Yeah, me too, I guess." I giggled.

"Speaking of fun," Mom continued. "I had an idea that I wanted to run by you."

"Okay, I'm all ears," I said. "You know, I feel like I could sit and talk with you for hours." Mom and I both burst out laughing at that one.

"Okay, we'll return to the topic of young love at another time," Mom said. "Right now I want to talk to you about the new bedroom project you and Allie have been working on."

"*That's* 'speaking of fun'?" I snarked. "Mom,

this could be serious. You might need to go to the doctor to get your fun meter adjusted."

"Clever, Sam," Mom replied. "I am well aware that cleaning out your rooms hasn't been fun for you two. So here's my proposal. I'm not going to be able to dig out from the pile of papers I've been buried under for a while. But once this project is finished, I'll have a lot more free time on my hands. And that's where these come in. . . ."

Mom opened up her night table, pulled out a stack of magazines, and spread them out on the bed. They were all glossy and printed on really beautiful paper (sorry, I just can't let it go)— magazines like *Elle Decor*, *House Beautiful*, and *Home and Design*.

"Are you giving me an assignment?" I asked. "Write an article about the horrors of cleaning your room to pitch to one of these magazines?"

"No, but that's not a bad idea, if you're up for it," Mom said. "I am giving you a different kind of assignment. It's a redesign partnership. These magazines are just a start. You and Allie should use them as a springboard to build a plan for redesigning your rooms. You know, cut out pictures of furniture you like, collect swatches of colors and patterns that we could use, stuff like that. When you've got a good idea of what you want, we'll work together after school and on the weekends to make it come to life."

"A new bedroom?" I cried. "Thanks, Mom. That would be awesome." I love my room, but it's probably time to get rid of the curtains that have little bows on them. I started thinking about bedrooms I've seen on TV or in the movies that were really cool and looked like you'd want your friends to hang out there with you. "So," I said, "do you think maybe in the next few months we could do this?"

Mom gave me a hug and kissed the top of my head.

"Oh, Sam, I'm sorry you've been at the mercy of my schedule," she said. "I really am. I promise it will be within the next month. First things first: Clean them out so we have a fresh space to work with. Maybe you and Allie can spend some time together this weekend working on this project. You know, some big-sister-little-sister bonding?"

Now *that* was funny!

Chapter 2

SCHOOL REPORTER DROWNS IN A SEA OF PAPER

★ ★ ★

So I could fill you in on all the details of every minute that passed between the end of my conversation with Mom and my first Michael Lawrence sighting, but I don't want to drag you any deeper into the Martone pit of boredom. I will say that Allie was slightly more interested in talking to me face-to-face than usual, especially when she came in to critique the abysmal state of my room. That conversation lasted at least an hour. It may have been a record!

I could see Allie's point, though. As I've mentioned too many times, I have an attachment to paper. But when I started to take a look at all the paper that was scattered around my room, I could see how it might have started to get in the way. By the window there was a huge mound of old tests and homework that I wanted to sort so I could use them to study for finals, but I hadn't gotten around to that yet. There were printouts of article drafts I had proofread and revised, which could probably go in the trash but were still scattered on top of and underneath my desk. There were a few books piled up in stacks in every corner, maybe even more than a few, but definitely not a "plethora" like Allie said. She was just showing off a new SAT word she learned.

I could see the need for a change, and I made a note to handle it ASAP. (I actually wrote a note in my notebook, because I do not have a photographic memory like that supercute boy that I know.) But I'm going to fast-forward a few thousand minutes and focus on a much more pleasant image—the image of Michael Lawrence's eyes.

They appeared to have some magical hypnotizing powers, because I didn't realize that I was standing in front of my locker literally staring into Michael's azure eyes even while he was walking straight toward me.

"Hey, Sam. Everything okay?" Michael asked.

I sincerely hoped that my mouth was not wide open with drool hanging from it at that moment, but I knew it was a definite possibility. Total embarrassment.

"Oh, yeah, hi," I said, trying to send cool vibes to my burning cheeks. "Sorry. I was just spacing out, trying to remember what books I needed to bring to my first few periods."

"I hear you," Michael said. "It's definitely hard to get back into the swing of things after the weekend. Did you have a good one?"

"Me? It was great," I lied. "I caught up on some sleep, spent some time with my friends. How about you?"

"Mine definitely wasn't as fun as yours," Michael said. "My batting average has been a little low lately, so I was in the batting cage a lot, working on my swing. My muscles were so sore at the end of the first day, I wasn't sure if I could make it onto the field the next day."

Michael continued talking about baseball, but I couldn't tell you a word that he said because

I was still stuck on the word "muscles." When he said that word, I immediately glanced at his arms, and then I noticed how nice they looked all wrapped up in his tight sleeves. I wondered how it would feel to slip my hand into his hand. I wondered . . .

"Sam?" Michael asked. "Are you with me? I just said that I ran into a friend of yours at my baseball practice."

"What?" I said, trying to snap back to reality. "I don't have any friends who play baseball. Except for you, I mean."

"It was that Danny Stratham kid from West Hills," Michael said. "He said to tell you hello."

"He did?" I was surprised. "I hardly know him. I'm surprised he mentioned me."

"Well, he talks like you know each other pretty well," Michael said, his tone sounding a little less supercute than it had a few minutes ago. "He asked if you'd be coming to the Cougar baseball games."

"Oh yeah. I'm definitely planning to come to the games," I said.

"Well, if I see him again, I'll let him know." Michael huffed.

"No, don't tell him. . . ," I started to explain.

Just then, the bell for first period rang, and Michael turned and walked away. Our classes were in different directions, so I couldn't even catch up to him and finish my sentence.

Four periods went by and I still hadn't seen Hailey anywhere. I really needed to talk to her. I wanted to ask her what she thought about the whole Michael Lawrence situation. I knew she was the only person in the world who could feel my pain at fumbling that conversation so badly.

Finally, the lunch bell rang. I threw my stuff into my locker and ran over to Hailey's. "Hey, Hails. I really need to talk to you."

Hailey looked up at me for the first time since I had arrived at her locker. Which was strange. I wanted to shout, "Hello, BFF here; remember me? You need to direct your attention *my* way."

Instead, Hailey grabbed her lunch and put her hand on my arm, like you would do to a stranger if you wanted to show them some sympathy. Just then I realized that Anthony, the student council president, was standing next to her. Hailey is the vice president.

"I'm sorry, Sam. I really want to catch up, but Anthony and I have a big student government event this week," Hailey explained. "We need to do some hard-core planning at lunch and after school this week. I'll call you later, okay?"

Then Hailey and Anthony hurried down the hall. Away from me, even though I was heading to the cafeteria too.

It's okay, guys. I can take a hint.

I slogged toward the lunchroom, feeling confused and rejected. Hailey and Anthony were huddled in a corner, busy "hard-core planning." Michael waved at me when I walked in, but he was sitting with some guys on the baseball team, and I didn't want them to catch me accidentally gazing into Michael's deep blue eyes.

I realized that I wasn't even hungry anymore. In fact, I felt a little queasy. So I took my lunch back to my locker and headed to the newsroom to check in with Mr. Trigg. He's the advisor of the

Cherry Valley Voice, the school newspaper. He takes the advisor role pretty seriously and always has a lot of good advice for reporters like Michael and me. I wouldn't tell the rest of the staff this, but I'm pretty sure we're his favorites. He almost always gives us the best assignments to work on together. And he gave me the top-secret job of writing the Dear Know-It-All column. I give advice to my schoolmates, and no one even knows it's me. I admit, it's pretty satisfying when I hear everyone talking about what good advice Dear Know-It-All gives.

Mr. Trigg was posting a quote above the computer bank in the newsroom. It said, "The truth is incontrovertible, malice may attack it, ignorance may deride it, but in the end; there it is."

"Let me guess—Churchill." I laughed.

It was a no-brainer. Everyone at Cherry Valley knew that Mr. Trigg was obsessed with Winston Churchill.

"Correct, Martone," Mr. Trigg answered. "And for that brilliant conjecture, you receive today's top prize."

"Wow, what's that?" I asked.

Mr. Trigg hurried into his office and returned with a folder filled with—you guessed it—paper.

"Here you go. Some new letters to Dear Know-It-All, all vetted by your trusty advisor," Mr. Trigg said. "I hope your weekend was restful and that you have renewed vigor to apply to your newspaper work."

"Oh yes, I've got loads of vigor." I chuckled. "I can't wait to get to work."

"So happy to hear that!" Mr. Trigg cheered. "I know you'll be coming to our staff meeting on Friday, but I was hoping you'd consider accepting an assignment before then. The student government event is on Wednesday, and I'll need a reporter to cover it. Would you be able to do it?"

"Sure, I'd love to," I replied. "Will I be working alone?"

Please say no. . . . Please say no. . . . Please say no. . . . Please say no. . . .

"I hadn't considered it, honestly," Mr. Trigg said. "But if you'd like to rope in Mr. Lawrence to assist you, that's fine with me."

Thank you. . . . Thank you. . . . Thank you. . . .
Thank you. . . . Thank you. . . .

"Great," I said. "I'll get started reading these letters and choosing one for the next issue. And I'll ask Michael if he's available to help with the story. If not, I'll just fly solo."

"Sounds like an excellent plan, Martone," Trigg said. "I have the greatest confidence in your abilities."

"Thank you, Mr. Trigg," I said. "I can't wait to get started."

I really couldn't, honestly. First, and best, it gave me another opportunity to work with Michael. And now Hailey would *have* to talk to me if she wanted her big event to be covered in the newspaper.

I didn't see either Hailey or Michael the rest of the day, and when I got home I had so much homework that it was nearly dinnertime when I finished. Allie stopped in my room after dinner to give me some pictures she had cut out for me. I appreciated the help, but Allie and I are so different, it was hard to believe we shared any

DNA. Our tastes were nothing alike. She likes glitzy and flashy; I like design that is simple and low-key. She did have some clever ideas for cool filing systems and bookshelves, and even better, for stenciling words and quotes on the walls, so I put those in a folder and took out the folder of Dear Know-It-All letters. The first few were as boring as my weekend had been. Then I read a couple that weren't going to work for other reasons.

Dear Know-It-All,

Are skinny jeans still in? Do you think it's okay if I wear boot-cut jeans to school sometimes, or will I be showing everyone that I have no fashion sense?

—Denim Dummy

Obviously one student at Cherry Valley had no idea that *I* was Dear Know-It-All, and also didn't know that it was an *advice* column, not a *fashion* column.

Dear Know-It-All,

Can you like more than one boy at the same time? Would you keep it a secret, or would you let them both know how you feel? Don't you think keeping it a secret is unfair?

<3 X 2

That one was interesting, but I didn't feel like I could answer it without careful consideration, and I didn't want writing the Dear Know-It-All column to take up all my time for this issue. I had a lot of homework, a heavy test schedule coming up, and a room to redecorate. Maybe Mom could help with the answer, I thought, smiling to myself. I put the letter on the top of the pile just in case I changed my mind and decided to read the rest later.

I was in the middle of my getting-ready-for-bed routine when I realized that Hailey had never called me like she said she was going to. I wasn't going to give her the satisfaction of texting or calling her now, after she had blown me off at lunch. I started to get upset about it, and then I remembered my sleep routine. If I went to bed stressed out, I would never be able to fall asleep. I wasn't sure exactly what would help, but Mom always says that it's important to get your feelings off your chest, so I figured I'd write an e-mail about how I felt to Hailey; I just wouldn't send it.

Hey, Hailey,

Did you get amnesia and forget that you had a best friend? You haven't called or texted me since Friday, and you hardly even looked at me today. I know you're busy, but you would think you could spare a couple of minutes to talk to me, considering how many hours I devote to tutoring you.

Feeling forgotten,
Sam

It was incredible, but I actually felt better after I wrote it all down. I got into bed and tried to focus on the fact that tomorrow I would get to ask Michael to work with me on the new story. It was going to be a great day, whether Hailey wanted to be a part of it or not.

Chapter 3

MARTONE'S BEST FRIEND IS MISSING IN ACTION

★ ★ ★

I was going to look for Michael as soon as I finished putting my books in my locker the next morning, but I didn't have to. I heard a knock on my locker door and turned around to see him looking even better than he had the day before, if that was possible.

He leaned in and put his arm over my head, propping himself up against my locker and coming in close to talk to me. It had been difficult to concentrate on our conversation yesterday. Now it was nearly impossible.

"Hey, Pasty," Michael said, so close that his voice was vibrating on my face. "Do you have a minute? I wanted to ask you something about the *Voice*."

"Perfect," I said, trying to stay composed. "I have something to ask you about the *Voice* too."

"Okay, you go first," he said.

"No, you go first. . . . Oh, forget it," I mumbled. "Mr. Trigg asked me to cover the big student government event on Wednesday. Want to help?"

"The Green Team?" Michael asked. "Sure, I'd like to work on that story. You might have to take on more of the reporting, though. Between baseball practice and homework, I don't have a lot of spare time. Is that okay?"

"I can do that," I said. "But what do you mean, the Green Team?"

"I figured your best bud, Hailey, already told you all about it." Michael laughed. "That's the big 'secret' event they have planned. Anthony and Hailey have started a Green Team, and they're going to talk about ways that students can work together to make the school more environmentally friendly."

"Oh, *that* Green Team," I said, trying to cover. "I think Hailey mentioned it, but I was too busy with other stuff to pay attention. Anyway, what's your question?"

"It's not a big deal; just forget it," Michael said.

"Come on. That's not fair," I said. "Spill."

"I just had a question about Dear Know-It-All," Michael said.

"Why would you think I would be able to answer it?" I asked.

I had always suspected that Michael was onto my Dear Know-It-All identity, and it looked like he might be ready to put me on the spot right now. I had promised Mr. Trigg that I would never reveal to anyone my work on the column, even my closest friends. Even Hailey. Only Mr. Trigg and my mom knew. Help!

"I don't know, just a suspicion that you might have some pull with Mr. Trigg," Michael asked.

"Now you're really confusing me," I said.

"I'm sorry, it's . . . it's really dumb," Michael stammered. "And I'm not even asking for me. . . . It's for a friend."

"Of course," I said. "So what does your friend want to know?"

"Oh, well he—I mean she—was wondering if it would be possible to get a letter back after it was submitted. You know, privately, between the letter writer and Dear Know-It-All. Before it was put in the *Voice*."

"Gee, Michael. I honestly don't know the answer," I said. "Maybe your friend will get lucky. Dear Know-It-All only answers one letter an issue. Your friend's letter might never even get published. But I can ask Mr. Trigg if you don't want to."

"That's okay, but thanks," Michael said. "I think she just regretted what she wrote after she had time to think about it."

"Well, it's all anonymous, so the good news is that even if it does get into the *Voice*, no one will ever know that she wrote it."

"Yeah, I'll remind her of that," he said. "So do you want to meet at lunchtime to go over questions we have about the Green Team story?"

"Sounds like a plan," I said.

Michael was still leaning against the locker, and he leaned in a little closer so that his cheek was brushing against my hair. Was it an accident? I held my breath. I wondered if he could smell my shampoo. I think it smelled pretty good, like strawberries.

"Later, Pasty," he whispered before walking away.

I would have collapsed into a puddle on the hallway floor, but I knew I couldn't risk being the talk of the lunchroom, especially today. What was up with that, though?

I've known Michael since kindergarten, and while he's always been absolutely adorable, he's also always been a supernice guy. Sometimes I think he likes me. And sometimes I think he forgets I exist. It gets complicated.

But did he just kind of try to whisper in my ear? That's so not Michael's style. A smooth operator like Danny Stratham, sure. Michael Lawrence, definitely not. He's the type of guy who will bake you cinnamon buns and then offer you a napkin to wipe the icing off your mouth and not look at you like you're a total loser because you totally have a big glob of icing on your upper lip. Not that I'm complaining. Michael Lawrence can whisper in my ear any day. It was just going to be really difficult to concentrate on anything else for the rest of the day—maybe even all week. Maybe all month. And I didn't even know if my best friend would have time to analyze every detail like we usually would. She still hadn't called or stopped by my locker to see me. I guess the Green Team was more important than our team.

At lunch, Michael waved and pointed to the seat next to him. I made sure to sit on the opposite side of the table. I think we had enough close contact for one day.

"Wouldn't it be easier to write notes if we were sitting next to each other?" Michael asked.

"Not a problem," I said. "I am excellent at reading upside down."

"Another talent that I was unaware of." Michael laughed. "Impressive, Pasty."

"I know. I try to keep it on the DL," I said. "I don't want everyone to know about my secret skill."

Michael smiled at me, and thankfully it was the good old, warm, friendly Michael Lawrence smile that made me feel comfortable and happy.

Hopefully he had gotten all the leaning and whispering out of his system earlier.

"So what do you know about Green Team?" I asked him. "Because I haven't seen much of Hailey lately, and I don't really know what they're planning."

"I noticed," Michael admitted. "I saw you leave the cafeteria the other day without eating when Hailey was busy with Anthony. You could have come sit with us."

"And talk about pop flies and cleats?" I laughed. "Thanks, but I'd rather talk to Mr. Trigg."

"Okay, fair enough," Michael said. "But just for the record, I am your friend. You can sit at my table any day."

"The record is noted," I answered. "And if I smell cinnamon buns, you can count me in."

Michael laughed. "The last time I brought cinnamon buns to school, the guys from the team ripped them out of my hands before I could even get to the cafeteria, so I think I'll only be serving them in my kitchen from now on."

"Great, then you'll have to invite me over the

next time you make them," I said.

Wait a minute! Did I just say that? *Martone Requests Invite to Crush's Kitchen, Waits for Rejection.*

"Of course, but it probably won't be until after baseball season," Michael replied. "I don't have a lot of free time these days."

Ugh! He totally thought I was inviting myself over. Way to go, Martone.

"No problem. I didn't really mean you have to invite me over," I started, embarrassed, and then it was like I just couldn't stop. "I mean, if you wanted to, I wouldn't say no, but you really don't have to. You can even just give me the recipe and I'll make my own. I'm pretty—"

"Calm down, Pasty," Michael said. "I knew what you meant. Let's leave the cinnamon buns in the kitchen and talk about this Green Team meeting."

"Good idea," I said. "The meeting is tomorrow, after school. I know that Anthony and Hailey have been disappointed because not a lot of kids have been coming to the student government meetings."

"Well, it *is* student government," Michael said. "What do they expect? They're competing with a lot of other after-school activities too, like baseball and the play."

"It's true," I admitted. "But not everyone is on a sports team or in the play. I think only ten kids showed up to their last meeting, and one of them was a reporter for the *Voice*."

"So tomorrow there will be *two* reporters." Michael laughed. "That should help."

"I don't know if Hailey would agree." I laughed too. "But let's figure out what we want to find out there."

As usual, Michael just sat and talked and listened while I scribbled frantically in his notebook. I wondered what it would be like to have a photographic memory. One thing that would be totally awesome: I could replay word for word every conversation I had ever had with Michael Lawrence. Even something that might seem boring to someone listening in could be thrilling to me. There was always just a tiny detail about the way he raised his voice when he added, "Right,

Pasty?" to the end of a statement that made it seem like he was talking about so much more than just writing a story. It was the type of subtle clue that you wanted to rehash a thousand times with your best friend. "Do you think he just meant, 'We'll find out tomorrow, right, Pasty?' because we're going to the meeting, or do you think there was something deeper behind it?" Hailey would listen to me go on and on and she wouldn't even seem annoyed by it. If she were around to listen to me go on and on, which of course she wasn't.

After our lunch meeting, I was secretly hoping I would bump into Hailey in the halls so I could give her the cold shoulder and show her how it felt to be snubbed by your best friend. No such luck. It was like Hailey had disappeared from the halls of Cherry Valley Middle School. On the way home from school, I turned off my phone, then turned it back on again, sure that I must have missed a call or a text from Hailey and this was all just a big misunderstanding. Nada.

I moped into the house, so frustrated that I even slammed the door behind me—really loudly.

Usually Mom would be all over me for that, but she was so wrapped up in some tax dilemma that I just heard her groan. Great, I'm not even worthy of the attention it would take Mom to reprimand me.

At least Allie seemed to realize that I was alive. She ran down the stairs, her hands full of fabric swatches.

"Sam, I'm so glad you're home," Allie cooed. "I hope you don't mind, but I've been checking out some samples in your room, and I think I've found the perfect ones."

"Um, hold on a minute, okay? I think I need to put on some sunglasses first," I said snarkily.

The colors might have been trendy, but they were hard for me to look at—a green so bright that a lime would have been jealous; metallic patterns that looked like an optical illusion; and a hideous fuchsia, orange, and turquoise combination that might have been inspired by a melted bowl of rainbow sherbet.

"Here's a little advice, Sam," Allie said, obviously not happy with my reply. "When people are trying to help you, you should act appreciative and grateful, even if you're not."

"I'm sorry, Allie," I said, and I was. "Some things have been bothering me lately, and I took it out on you. I do appreciate that you're helping me. It's been a rough week."

"Oh, is it the Hailey thing?" Allie asked.

"How do you know about the Hailey thing?" I gasped. "Uh, I mean, *what* Hailey thing?"

"Sam, just because you *think* I'm not paying attention doesn't mean that I'm not actually paying attention," Allie said. "Hailey's usually the first person you talk to when you get home from school, if she's not actually here."

"She's just busy with school stuff," I said. "It's not a big deal."

"Okay, if you say so," Allie said. "But believe it or not, I know what it's like to have a fight with your best friend, and it really hurts. So if you want to talk, I'll listen."

"There's nothing to talk about." I laughed, trying to look less upset than I actually was. "There's no fight. Everything will be fine as soon as this Green Team stuff is done."

And when those words came out of my mouth, I really believed that they were sort of true. Hailey and I have been best friends for as long as I've known her. I didn't think anything could ever change that. I had no idea how wrong I was, but I would find out soon enough.

Chapter 4

FRIENDSHIP GOES UP IN BLAZES, CASUALTIES ALL AROUND

★ ★ ★

There are some things that you never really expect to happen. Like, you never expect your big sister to suddenly turn insightful and friendly and helpful after she's spent most of your life either taunting you or ignoring you. And now, when I think about it, I realize that maybe there's a price you have to pay when a remarkably positive turnaround like that happens. Maybe something equally as negative has to balance it out. It makes sense if I think about it enough. What doesn't make sense is that the negative would be something as horrific as having your best friend turning against you.

The concept is so horrific that it's difficult for me to write about it, and writing is something that always comes incredibly easy to me. But every time I think about the fact that Hailey Jones, the person I have shared every secret with for as long as I can remember, would not just ignore me, but would do something that she knew would be hurtful to me, it makes a ball of sadness and anxiety and queasiness start to rise from my stomach and travel up my throat. I've cried a lot since the Green Team meeting earlier today, so much that I would think I didn't have any tears left, but just typing her name makes me start to well up again.

Anyway, I am a reporter, and it's a reporter's duty to report the facts in an unbiased manner, without letting emotions get in the way, so I will report what happened first. And I apologize in advance, because I'm pretty sure that an emotion or two is going to sneak in there anyway.

Today, Wednesday, was just like Monday and Tuesday. I didn't hear from Hailey, didn't see her at the lockers in the morning, didn't catch a glimpse of her in the hallways during school. I saw her in the cafeteria at lunch, but she was sitting with Anthony Wright—of course—and didn't even look my way. Some of my friends from the newspaper asked me if I wanted to sit with them, but I couldn't stand the thought of sitting there and watching Hailey ignore me, so I just went to the library and did my homework. I figured that would give me more time after school to work on the Green Team story.

After last period, Michael met me by my locker and we walked into the auditorium. I know Hailey and Anthony had worked really hard at publicizing the event—there were Green Team posters hanging all over school—but when we entered the auditorium, you could still hear our footsteps echoing through the room. It was definitely a better turnout than usual. There might have even been fifty kids there. Still, I knew Hailey was hoping for the whole school, so I felt a little bad for her and Anthony and decided that I would try to make the Green Team sound really important in the article. Maybe if my article helped Hailey's Green Team, she would have more time to spend with me.

Anthony Wright went up to the podium and

started to speak. Anthony is a great guy, and he has good ideas for improving the school, but his public speaking skills can still use a little work. If the *idea* of the Green Team wasn't appealing to most students, hearing Anthony speak about it wasn't going to convince them otherwise. He did a good job of outlining the mission of the team and explaining the work that he and Hailey had already done to get started, but if I weren't a reporter intently taking notes on what he was saying, it might have just sounded like *"Green Team, blah blah blah, environmental responsibility, blah blah blah, student activism, blah blah blah."*

I'm sorry. That's harsh and not particularly objective. Like I said, Anthony did a pretty good job giving an overview of the Green Team.

Then Hailey stepped up to the microphone. She's a lot more dynamic a speaker than Anthony is, and she seemed to be bursting with Green Team pride. I'm always proud of Hailey when she speaks at student government meetings, because even though the audience tends to be small, she does an amazing job at motivating them. I'm especially

proud because I know how much Hailey's dyslexia gets in the way of her schoolwork and how
easy it would be for her to just chalk up school as
a necessary evil on the road to future success as
a Team USA soccer star, but Hailey really defines
school spirit in these moments.

She told the students that they were looking
to start Green Team subcommittees. Each subcommittee would be responsible for researching
and implementing an environmental reform in the
school. Anthony was going to be heading up an
"SOS." The acronym stood for Styrofoam Out of
Schools, and their first mission would be to get the
Styrofoam trays taken out of our lunchroom and
replaced with a more environmentally friendly
option. It seemed like a worthy cause, and some of
the other students agreed. At least ten kids raised
their hands and signed on to help out.

Hailey continued by saying that they would
welcome ideas from anyone who wanted to start
a Green Team subcommittee and that they would
help them organize and sign up group members.
She said that the next Green Team meeting would

be in two weeks and at that meeting they would discuss subcommittee ideas. Finally, Hailey said that she would be closing the meeting by announcing her own subcommittee.

As I was scribbling notes, my feelings toward Hailey started to change, and I felt a little guilty that I had been angry that she wasn't around for me. Obviously, she had been really busy with this Green Team stuff. She'd put together a great presentation, and I think it was probably going to create a lot more interest in student government, too.

Michael was obviously thinking the same thing, because he leaned over and said, "Wow, Hailey and Anthony's work on Green Team is really impressive."

I nodded my head in agreement, eager to hear what Hailey was going to say next. I decided that I would probably sign up for her subcommittee. She could use the support, and even though I was busy, it would be a fun thing to do together.

And then Hailey presented her idea.

"My subcommittee is called GO GO," she said. "It stands for 'Get On Board, Go Online.'"

I didn't want to ruin Hailey's moment, so I didn't say that GO GO was wrong—"Get On Board, Go Online" means her acronym really should have been "GOB GO," which wasn't as cute or catchy.

"Are you aware of how much paper is used by our school every time they print a new issue of the *Cherry Valley Voice*?" Hailey asked. "How much energy goes into making that paper? How many trees have been cut down to produce one single issue, which you probably throw into your trash can when you get home?"

Wh-wh-what? There is no way I just heard Hailey say what she said. I looked at Michael, and he looked just as shocked. He shrugged his shoulders and mimed writing on paper to signal that I should just keep taking notes. Which was a little problematic, because I realized that I had been holding my pencil so tightly while listening to Hailey that it had snapped in half.

I grabbed another pencil from my backpack and returned to taking notes, trying to remember that once upon a time, Hailey had been my best friend.

"There's an easy solution to the problem," Hailey continued. "Let's take the *Voice* into the twenty-first century. *Get on board* the GO GO subcommittee, and we'll help the *Voice* go online! We'll save paper, we'll save trees, and we'll save money that the school can use for even more important things, like equipment for the sports teams."

That was a low blow. Hailey knew almost everyone in school cared more about the sports teams than they did about the newspaper.

Hailey finished her speech by giving some statistics about carbon dioxide emissions and comparisons between printed papers and their digital equivalent. When she was done, at least twenty kids raised their hands to join GO GO. Unbelievable! My best friend was determined to destroy one of the most important things in the world to me, and she didn't even seem to care.

As everyone shuffled out of the auditorium, I just sat there, speechless. Michael looked at me and laughed nervously.

"This should make for an interesting story, right, Pasty?" he asked.

I didn't even know how to answer, because just then I looked up and saw Hailey heading my way.

"Hey, Sam. I'm sorry," she said. "I was planning to fill you in on all of this, but I was so busy with Anthony getting ready for this meeting, I just never got a chance."

"Oh, yeah, of course," I replied. "It had nothing to do with the fact that you're destroying my hopes and dreams . . . my reason for living."

I think Hailey thought I was joking.

"Funny, Sam." Hailey laughed. "That's hardly true. The *Voice* will still be published, just digitally. Everyone will be able to read it online whenever they want. It's so convenient. No more lugging the paper around, crushing it into the bottom of your backpack, finding it three weeks later."

"I don't crush the *Voice*," I said, my face getting hot. "I read it. But I forgot. Of course you don't understand the value of the printed word. You don't even like to read, I guess because it's so hard for you!"

I could tell my verbal arrow hit the mark,

because Hailey's eyes immediately showed the hurt she felt. Even Michael gasped.

"That was uncalled for, Sam," Hailey said sadly. "I was worried that you might act like this. You are so self-involved sometimes. You can never see that anyone else might have a point of view that's different from your own."

"Are you kidding me, Hailey? I'm so self-involved?" I gasped. "Miss Watch-Me-Run-Around-the-Soccer-Field-I'm-Such-a-Gifted-Athlete-and-You're-Such-a-Klutz."

Michael put his hand on my arm.

"Sam, let's go back to the newsroom and go over our notes," he said. "We can compare our feelings about the proposal."

"Yeah, Pasty, that should make you happy," Hailey hissed. "Spend a little time sharing feelings with your favorite crush . . . I mean . . . co-reporter."

My face had been hot before; now it was on fire. I grabbed my backpack and ran out of the auditorium. I didn't stop until I reached my front door. I didn't want Hailey, or Michael, to see me cry. Not only was I about to lose the *Voice*, but I had lost my best friend, too. Hailey and I have had our disagreements before, but this was much more than a disagreement. Hailey had declared war on the *Cherry Valley Voice*, and that means she had just declared war on me.

I knew if Mom heard me come in crying she would want to talk, and I really wasn't ready to talk about what had happened yet. I quietly entered the kitchen and mumbled, "Hey, Mom," and she mumbled back to me. Luckily, Allie was in her room with her headphones on, probably listening to some motivational designer talk about transforming your life through the magic of the colors that surround you. Blech!

I put my backpack on my chair, closed the door, and changed into pajamas. I knew it was only three thirty p.m., but I wasn't planning on going anywhere. I figured I could always use the "I'm not feeling so hot" excuse if Mom asked, but considering how busy with work she was, she probably wouldn't ask anyway. I had already done my homework, so I crawled under my comforter, rolled into a ball, and sobbed softly so Mom couldn't hear me.

I wished that Hailey had never been elected to student government. I wished that I had chosen someone else to be best friends with. I wished that I could go back to the newsroom and tell Mr. Trigg that I didn't want to work on the Green Team story. But most of all, I wished that both Hailey and I could take back the things that we had said to each other, because I was worried that things would never be the same between us again.

Chapter 5

LIFE DOESN'T RETURN TO NORMAL AT CHERRY VALLEY

★ ★ ★

I must have cried myself to sleep, because I woke up to the sound of the phone ringing and Allie shouting, "Sam!"

I looked at my alarm clock and it said 7:00. Panic time! I had slept through the night without even realizing it, and I was going to be late for school! I threw on some leggings and a T-shirt, grabbed my backpack, and ran downstairs. As soon as I looked at the table and the sky outside the kitchen window, I could see my mistake. There was a box and three plates on the table. Two of the plates had pizza crust on them and a third was clean. The sun outside the window was setting in the sky, not rising. It was seven p.m.! I hadn't slept the whole night. I had just taken a really long nap.

I felt disoriented and fuzzy, and that feeling didn't get better when Allie asked, "What are you doing, Sam?"

"I'm just going to have some pizza," I said, rubbing the sleep out of my eyes. "I wasn't feeling well before. I guess I fell asleep."

"Okay, that's fine," Allie said. "But what about the phone?"

Allie waved the receiver around in the air. Right, the phone. It had rung, and Allie had called me. That must mean the phone call was for me. My brain cells were obviously not fully awake yet. Duh.

Allie put her hand over the receiver and whispered loudly, "It's Michael."

Great. I couldn't get out of talking to him now. He had probably heard everything Allie and I said to each other before that. I grabbed the receiver and walked into the hall.

"Hello?" I said, trying to not sound like I had just woken up.

"Hey, Sam," Michael said. "I just wanted to check and make sure you're okay."

"I'm okay," I replied. "Why, is something wrong?"

"Oh, well, you know, everything that happened today in the meeting," he stammered. "And then I tried texting you, and I called your cell a couple of times, and I started to get worried when you didn't answer."

I unzipped my backpack and took out my cell phone. Sure enough, I had missed texts *and* phone calls from Michael. It figured. It was that kind of a day.

"Sorry. I just got busy and I forgot to take my phone out of my backpack," I answered. "I'm fine, really."

"I don't think Hailey was trying to hurt you with her idea," Michael said. "It's not like other newspapers haven't gone digital."

"Thank you for saying that. I disagree, though," I replied. "I think Hailey knew exactly what she was doing. It's fine. I don't really care anymore."

"Of course you care," Michael said. "You're best friends."

"Were best friends," I corrected him. "Not are. I don't even know if we're friends at all anymore."

"That's pretty drastic, don't you think?" Michael asked.

I never would have imagined that I would want a conversation with Michael to end, but this one needed to, badly. I was already on the verge of tears again, and I didn't want Michael to be on the other end of my latest sob fest.

"Maybe it is, maybe it isn't," I said. "I don't really want to talk about it. We have an article to write and a paper to save. Are you in or out?"

"I'm in, Pasty." Michael laughed. "We'll talk more tomorrow. I just wanted to make sure you were okay, and obviously you are."

"I am," I said. "I'll see you tomorrow. Bye."

I hung up the phone and turned to find Allie looking at me suspiciously.

"Is everything okay?" she asked.

I know Allie was being nicer to me lately, but

I didn't want to cry in front of her, either. So I didn't. I snapped.

"WHY DOES EVERYONE KEEP ASKING ME THAT?" I screamed. "I'LL BE FINE IF YOU ALL JUST LEAVE ME ALONE!"

I grabbed my backpack and started to storm back up to my room. Then I turned around, grabbed two slices of pizza, plopped them on a plate, and stormed up to my room. All that sobbing can make a girl hungry.

I heard Mom come out of her office and Allie whisper something like, "I don't know, maybe puberty hormones." I almost turned back around to throw my pizza at her, but decided it was better not to start another fight at the moment.

I was annoyed, but I couldn't help but laugh when I caught a glimpse of myself in the mirror.

"Gee, Martone, that would have been awkward," I said to myself as I realized that I had been planning to rush to school with uncombed hair, a pair of leggings that had a juice stain on the front of them, and a T-shirt that I had outgrown six months ago. Allie would have definitely disowned me if that had happened. Ugh, plus my eyes were red and puffy. I totally looked like I had been crying.

I sat in front of the computer. I was definitely not emotionally ready to start on the Green Team story. I didn't even want to think about what had happened today. I figured I could make a dent in the Dear Know-It-All column and put my mind on someone else's problems. I almost wished that I could have written myself a letter about what happened with Hailey. But that would have been too obvious. Besides, I wouldn't have a clue how to answer it.

Mr. Trigg had forwarded me some Dear Know-It-All e-mails that he had reviewed, so I started to read through them. One of them was a topic I hadn't gotten before.

Dear Know-It-All,

I have a sweater that my grandmother knit for me. She made it a few years ago, when I didn't care about fashion so much. It is definitely NOT a fashion statement. I used to wear it all the time, but now that I'm getting older, I'm worried that it's not such a good fit anymore. (It fits fine; you know what I mean.) I'm torn, because I feel good when I wear it. It makes me feel close to her, and it's so comfortable. Could the sweater and I have outgrown each other? Should I give it to someone else and move on?

-A Tight Fit

I looked around my room. Allie had placed sticky notes on almost every item in it. An X meant that I should throw it away. A plus sign meant that I should keep it. A question mark meant that Allie didn't know what to do with it.

But there were some X's that I wasn't sure I was ready to give up yet. I wasn't even sure I was ready to give up the way my room looked anyway. I know Mom was excited about redecorating, and I was, too, but now I looked around and saw that my room was full of memories. Allie had put a lot of X's on my paper piles, and there was a big X on the bulletin board that was splattered with ridiculous headlines like *Jellyfish Apocalypse Not Coming* and *Alien Baby Looks*

Like Katy Perry. I knew that the bulletin board wasn't the most stylish thing in the room, and that it wasn't even particularly necessary, but it made me even sadder to think about losing it when I remembered that Hailey had contributed at least five of the headlines. That was when she was a real best friend, when she knew how much I cared about newspapers and had taken the time to cut out funny headlines for me. Now she just wanted to banish them forever.

The letter made me think about Hailey, too. Was I like a grandma-knit sweater that she had outgrown? Maybe this was just her way of sabotaging our friendship so she could move on to some new, improved best friend. I mean, I was part of the twenty-first century, too. It was a little hard to avoid that, considering it was the century we were living in. But I didn't think that being modern meant getting rid of everything from the past. I read books on my tablet, but sometimes I still wanted to curl up with a real book, to feel the pages flip through my fingers, to fold a page over and then find my spot later. I didn't think there was anything wrong with that.

I decided that the grandma-sweater letter would be my choice for this issue's column, and I sent Mr. Trigg a quick e-mail to get his approval. He usually trusted my instincts, so I didn't think it would be a problem. I typed a few notes about how I might respond to the letter and then shut my computer down.

Because of my extralong nap, I wasn't very tired and I didn't think my sleep routine was going to help, so I decided to exert some energy and start going through some of the piles in my room. Some of the things that had an X on them were definitely destined for the trash, like the piles of article drafts and old homework.

Others I wasn't sure about yet. There were books that I could donate because I knew I'd never read them again and books that I was sure I'd never part with because I wanted to read them over and over again, but there was another group of books that I just liked having around, even though I wasn't sure if I'd ever get back to them. I'm sure Allie would talk me into getting rid of them, too, but it wasn't a decision I was ready to make on my own, so I put them in a Maybe box.

Other things in the Maybe box included tickets to the movies Hailey and I had gone to together, flyers from school sports events (the ones Michael had participated in), article drafts with Mr. Trigg's comments on them, and printouts of photos that I had stored digitally on my computer.

I had already filled two recycling bags with paper, so I carried them down to put them in the recycling can outside.

"I'm impressed," Allie said. "I didn't think you'd ever throw out even one piece of paper."

Allie was at the kitchen counter, packing some snacks for tomorrow's lunch.

"Me either," I confessed. "I'm still not ready for a clean sweep. I have a big Maybe box."

"I have an idea," Allie said. "Why don't you leave your Maybe box with me? If it's not too personal, I mean. I might have a different perspective on the stuff."

"Supposedly I'm not very good at seeing different perspectives," I said.

"Who said that?" Allie asked. "Some teacher?"

"No, and I don't want to talk about it," I said. "I'll put the Maybe box in your room. You can do whatever you want with it."

"You're really coming along, Sammy-pants," Allie said.

She knew that I hated when she called me that. She didn't care, obviously. I didn't either right now, having heard worse from my best friend.

"What about colors?" Allie asked. "Did you like any of my ideas?"

"No offense, Allie-baba," I said, hitting back with the nickname that she wasn't fond of. "But I'm not as 'colorful' a person as you are. I'd rather go with something more neutral. Maybe black and white. Like a newspaper."

"How bold," Allie said. "That's never been done before."

"Whatever." I sighed. "If you want to help, fine. If not, I don't care."

"I think you need another nap," Allie retorted.

"Maybe," I said.

I grabbed a handful of carrot sticks and went

back upstairs. I carried my Maybe box into Allie's room and then changed back into my pajamas. My room was already starting to look more organized. I tried to focus on that and not my fight with Hailey so I could go back to sleep. Because I knew if I thought about Hailey, I'd be up all night.

Chapter 6

BEST FRIEND BATTLE, ROUND TWO, NO WINNER DECLARED

★ ★ ★

I was hoping that the equation of my late-afternoon nap, together with a full night's sleep, plus waking up in a less-cluttered room, would add up to yesterday's events seeming less devastating than they had the day before. You know how sometimes when you're in the middle of something and it seems like the biggest crisis that has ever happened to you, and then you look back on it later and you think, "I was freaking out about not getting chosen to be editor in chief, but it gives me time to do all the other things I want to do."

Okay, well, that wasn't a particularly good

example. But I was hoping that maybe I'd wake up and realize that it was all a very bad dream caused by too much sleep. No such luck.

I was bombarded with evidence of Hailey's backstabbing as soon as I walked through the doors of school. She had posted signs for the GO GO subcommittee everywhere. I knew she was doing it deliberately, to rub my nose in it, because I didn't see many signs for Anthony's SOS group. Michael was standing under a sign that was posted right next to my locker.

"I'm guessing you're not too happy right now," Michael said.

"It's fine," I said. "Two can play that game. I might start my own committee. POV. It stands for 'Print Our *Voice*.'"

"It's kinda catchy, Pasty," Michael said. "But not exactly your usual detached journalistic approach."

"Ugh." I groaned. "You're right. Maybe I should tell Mr. Trigg that I can't write the article. You can do it alone."

"No, I can't," Michael replied. "First, I don't

have time. And second, I don't think you really need to start a committee."

"But even if I don't, I won't be able to be detached," I said. "As you heard, I have trouble seeing a point of view that's different from my own."

"You know that's not true," Michael said. "And you also know that Hailey didn't mean it. You said something mean first."

"*I* said something mean first?" I said, shocked. "I think you need to check your photographic memory. Remember when Hailey said all that stuff about stopping the printing presses? I think that came first."

"Look, I don't want to get in the middle of this," Michael said. "It doesn't matter who said what first. We have a story to write, and we have to do it together."

"I'm not sure that I can be impartial," I admitted.

"It's okay. We can be impartial together," Michael suggested. "I know how you feel, so I'll try to lean the other way. Just don't take it personally."

I agreed, and we made a plan to meet at lunch-time again to divide up the work. I was really relieved that Michael acted professional about the story and hadn't brought up the whole "crush" comment. I can't believe Hailey had dared to go there. I shouldn't have been shocked, though, because it was obvious that I didn't really know Hailey at all.

Later that day Michael and I were sitting at a lunch table, talking about the people we might interview and some of the sources we might use for our research, when Hailey came marching over with her band of Green Team flunkies. She tossed a pile of printouts and pamphlets on the table. They all said things like "Save the Rainforest" and "Paper Free for You and Me."

Hailey acted like I was a ghost that she couldn't see.

"Michael, Mr. Trigg informed me that you are writing an article on the Green Team," Hailey said snippily. "I thought you might find this infor-mation useful."

"Thanks, Hailey," Michael replied. "I'm not

writing it by myself, though. Sam's my co-reporter."

"I am aware of that fact, and I've asked Mr. Trigg to reconsider and assign someone less biased to be your partner, but he refused," Hailey continued.

"WHA . . ." I was about to scream, but Michael kicked me under the table before it could escape from my mouth.

"I've worked with Sam a lot, and she's never been biased before," said Michael. "I'm sure she won't be now."

"I'm not so sure," Hailey replied. "But there's nothing I can do about it, so I'll just have to take your word. Happy writing."

Hailey turned so abruptly you could almost feel the disturbance in the air. I was certainly disturbed.

"What was that about?" I snapped.

"Hailey?" Michael asked. "She's trying to get the Green Team going. And get a couple of digs in on you."

"Digs?" I hissed. "More like poison darts. And anyway, that wasn't what I was talking about.

What was *that*?" I asked as I kicked him under the table.

"OW!" Michael yelped. "I didn't kick you that hard!"

"Why did you kick me at all?" I asked.

"I could see where it was heading," Michael said. "I didn't want you to say anything you'd regret later."

"Thanks, but I can take care of my mouth," I answered. "I mean, my words."

Michael laughed, and the sound of it immediately made me smile, despite how I annoyed I was by the kick.

"Take it easy, Sam," he said. "I'm on your side. I just really don't think the sides are as obvious as you think. I don't think Hailey's doing this to hurt you."

I opened my mouth in protest, but Michael cut me off.

"Let's go talk to Mr. Trigg," Michael suggested. "I want to hear how he feels about the GO GO thing."

"Now, that's the best idea you've had all day," I teased him. "A lot better than kicking me to keep me quiet."

The lunch bell rang, and we headed off in different directions to get to our classes. We agreed to meet in the newsroom after school. I got there first.

"Miss Martone, your friend Hailey stopped by to see me earlier today," Mr. Trigg greeted me.

"She's not my—," I started to answer.

"Yes, I gathered you two have had a spat," Mr. Trigg interrupted. "In any event, I'd like to know what you think about her proposal."

"That's funny. We were coming here to find out what you think," Michael said over my shoulder.

"That's a good question, Mr. Lawrence," Trigg complimented him. "But not nearly as important as what you think. You see, I'm from a different time. I have an emotional attachment to paper. It's what I've known all my life. So I admit my bias. I'm curious what you think, or more important, what you think your peers might think about it. Would they prefer a digital edition? Would they actually read it? Would any of them prefer paper?"

"I think the number of people who read the paper will drop," I said. "When we hand out the

Voice, everyone reads it at lunchtime and during study periods. When they're online, they have a million other distractions, e-mails, Websites to research, games to play. No one will ever take the time to read it."

"That might be true," Michael pointed out. "But Mr. Trigg is right. We need to find out what our peers think."

"We need to do a poll," I said, having a light-bulb moment.

"Brilliant!" Mr. Trigg cheered. "I knew I had chosen the right team for the story. Get to work!"

It was funny how Mr. Trigg could do that. Make you feel like the seeds that he planted were your own ideas, give you the boost of excitement you needed to take off and run with the story. I guess that's how good editors work. I wrote that in my notebook for future reference. I knew that if I could be unbiased about this story, if I could prove that my reporter skills outweighed my emotions, it would make Mr. Trigg see me in a new light.

Of course, that was put to the test as soon as I left the newsroom. Michael had to rush off to baseball practice, and I was at my locker packing up my books when Mrs. Brennan, the school's dean and guidance counselor, came to talk to me.

"Samantha, I'm glad I caught you," she said. "I was going to call you to my office today, but some other things got in the way."

I immediately felt my body stiffen. Usually when kids were called to Mrs. Brennan's office, it wasn't the best of news.

"Am I in trouble?" I asked nervously.

"No, no, it's not that," Mrs. Brennan said. "But do you have a couple of minutes to talk?"

"Sure," I replied. "Can I just text my mom to let her know I'll be a little late? I just told her I was heading home now."

"Of course," she said. "I'll wait."

I walked side by side with Mrs. Brennan to her office, but we didn't really talk much. I could see the few kids left in the hall staring, wondering what I had done wrong. I was thinking the same thing myself.

We got into the office, and Mrs. Brennan

gestured to the chair that was in front of her desk. I sat down.

"Samantha, you've always been an excellent student," Mrs. Brennan began. "I don't think I can remember a time when you weren't on honor roll or principal's list."

"Oh no!" I gasped. "Did I fail a test?"

"No!" Mrs. Brennan said. "Not that I know of, at least. I'm just wondering if you know how it might feel to not be so successful at school. To really have to struggle to keep up with your work."

"I have an idea," I said. "I have a friend—I mean, I know someone who has problems like that."

"I know you do," Mrs. Brennan said. "That's why I was so surprised to hear that you would bring something like that up in public, in school, in front of other people. As someone said, 'Call out their disability for the world to see.'"

"What?" I said, surprised. "I wouldn't do that. That's personal information. It's not something I would talk about."

"I don't think you intentionally did, Sam,"

Mrs. Brennan agreed. "And from what the other witnesses have said, you didn't specifically mention the disability."

"Witnesses?" I asked. "Are you sure I'm not in trouble?"

"I'm sure," Mrs. Brennan said. "Sometimes when we're friends with someone, we share a lot of things that we don't want other people to know about. I just want you to think about that. You're not in trouble, but I want you to think about how the things you say might affect others. I want you to think about how it might feel if you say something about someone who isn't able to read well, even if it wasn't intended to be hurtful."

Now I knew what Mrs. Brennan was talking about. Hailey! She was unbelievable! She went to Mrs. Brennan just because I said that she didn't like to read? I didn't say anything about her dyslexia, and almost everyone knew about that anyway because she got pulled out for reading intervention.

"Anyway, you're not in trouble. I know you're a great student and an asset to our school, but I just want you to think about the situation from another person's point of view," Mrs. Brennan said. "And if there are more problems, we may need to work this out some other way. But hopefully there won't be. Do you have any questions, Sam?"

"No, I understand perfectly, Mrs. Brennan," I said as I stood up to leave. "And believe me, I won't be saying a word about another person. Or, for that matter, to them."

Hailey had really gone too far now. She made it seem like I was the one who was insensitive. As if!

The one and only benefit of being called to Mrs. Brennan's office was that word spread like wildfire. I had just started walking home when Michael caught up to me.

"Pasty, wait." He huffed, out of breath.

"I thought you were at practice," I said.

"I was, but Coach let me leave early," Michael explained. "I said I had a big test tomorrow."

"Do you?" I asked.

"No. I heard you were with Mrs. Brennan," he admitted. "I wanted to make sure everything went okay."

"Everything?" I wondered.

"She called me into her office this morning," said Michael. "She asked me what happened after the Green Team meeting. I figured something was up. Does it have anything to do with Hailey?"

"Oh yeah, something's up," I agreed. "My former best friend is a traitor *and* a rat."

"Or maybe your former best friend's feelings were really hurt?" Michael suggested.

"Michael, are you trying to get all guidance counselor-y on me?" I said, half joking and half annoyed. "Because I had one of those sessions already today. And I'm aware that I need to take other people's 'point of view' into account."

"I definitely do not want to be *your* guidance counselor." Michael laughed. "That's way too much work."

"Ha-ha, you're funny," I snapped back. "Seriously, everything's fine."

"Great, then why don't you come over and we'll work on the article," Michael said. "I don't have time to make cinnamon buns, but I did call my mom and she said she can dig up some snacks for us. I told her you're always hungry," he said with a laugh.

"Now?" I asked. "I just told my mom I was coming home."

"Okay, I can walk you home and wait outside while you ask her," he said. "Then we can walk to my house together."

This was not the way I had imagined my afternoon would turn out. It was soooo much better! I was pretty sure Mom would say okay. She was so busy with work it wasn't like we would be spending much time together anyway.

I rushed into the house and knocked on Mom's office door.

"Finally, you're home," Mom said. "Is everything okay?"

"Better than okay, Mom," I said. "Do you think I could go over to Michael's house for a while? We're working on a big story for the *Voice*."

"Are his parents around?" Mom asked.

"Yes, his mother is home," I said. "You can call her if you have to."

"I trust you, Sam," Mom said. "Just make

sure you're home for dinner."

I raced upstairs, brushed my teeth, combed my hair, and then shook it out so it wouldn't look like I had just combed it. Then I ran back downstairs and walked outside, trying to look casual.

"That was fast," Michael noted. "Is it okay with your mom?"

"It's fine with her," I said. "She just wanted to make sure there would be 'adult supervision.'"

Michael laughed. "I know. My parents are the same way."

Michael and I spent the afternoon at his kitchen table. I tried not to roll my eyes when he took out the pile of printouts and pamphlets from Hailey.

"We need to be open to everyone's side," he said.

"I've been reminded of that before." I laughed. "A few times."

"I had an idea for how we might work on the story," Michael said. "I'll do the research about the benefits of digital publishing. You can handle the poll results and get some quotes from students who prefer paper. Next time we meet, we'll figure out how to put it all together."

"You're on a roll, Michael Lawrence," I noted.

"Actually, I taste better on rye bread," Michael joked. "With a little mustard."

His joke was so dumb I couldn't stop laughing.

"You should stick with journalism—or sports," I told him. "Because comedy is obviously not your thing."

"I've been told that before." He laughed. "A few times."

We started to come up with some poll questions, and then we cut the list to four questions because we knew students wouldn't spend a lot of time answering them. The four questions were:

Do you read the *Cherry Valley Voice* weekly?

yes/no

Do you read any newspapers online?

yes/no

Would you read the *Cherry Valley Voice* online?

yes/no

Would you prefer to read the *Voice* printed or online?

printed/online

We debated whether we should post the poll on Buddybook, but I thought that the results might be biased toward students who use the computer a lot. We decided to do a combination Buddybook poll along with a printed poll that students could fill out in the cafeteria at lunchtime.

I left Michael's feeling happier and more relaxed than I had all week. The proverb "Every cloud has a silver lining" seemed to be true for me. My Hailey cloud had turned into more time with Michael, and that was better than a silver lining—it was golden.

Chapter 7

MARTONE GETS THE BLAME . . . AGAIN

★ ★ ★

Mom and Allie were sitting at the kitchen table when I got home.

I was still smiling goofily when I joined them at the table.

"Productive meeting?" Mom asked.

"Very," I replied. "We wrote a poll that we're going to use for part of our article, and we're going to use the results as part of the article."

"Didn't you do that before?" Allie asked.

"We did, and it worked really well," I said. "So why mess with a good thing?"

"Speaking about messing with a good thing," Mom segued, "what is going on with Hailey?"

"What do you mean?" I asked, pretending to be oblivious.

"I ran into her mom when I went out to the

supermarket to pick up a chicken for dinner," Mom said. "She said Hailey's been just devastated by your fight and the hurtful things that you said."

"The hurtful things *I* said?" I snorted. "She keeps forgetting about the hurtful things *she* said. She just wants me to look like the bad guy."

"That happens a lot when good friends fight," Mom said. "It can be worse than a fight with a stranger, because friends know what's important to you, so they really know how to hurt you."

"Well, if that's what Hailey was going for, she definitely succeeded," I said. "She knows how important the *Voice* is to me, and she doesn't even care. Her Green Team is more important to her now than her best friend."

"Yes, her mother filled me in about her plan to try to put the paper online. Are you sure you aren't being overly sensitive, Sam?" Mom asked. "You and Hailey have been so close for so long. Do you really think it's worth giving up over something that's happening at school?"

"It's not just something that's happening at school," I said. "Hailey could have chosen a different Green Team topic. She didn't have to choose the newspaper. And she didn't even tell me first! She ignored me for a week and then announced it at the meeting! I don't know why she wanted to hurt me. I didn't do anything to her."

"I don't know the answer either, Sam," Mom said. "And I'm sorry I've been too busy to notice how you've been feeling. I just want you to know that I'm here if you want to talk about it."

"I'd rather not right now," I admitted. "I was kind of happy for a moment. You know the feeling, right, Mom? Like when you'd get a note from John."

"WHO'S JOHN?" Allie squealed.

My diversionary tactic worked. We spent the rest of dinner talking about Mom's love life and the letters I had found. Allie made Mom pull out the hatbox again, and we had a fun time teasing her about the romantic things her sweetheart John had written to her. I almost forgot about Hailey for the moment.

That's when I made my decision. I would purposefully forget about Hailey. I would forget that we were ever best friends. I would put the *Voice* and my commitment to unbiased reporting first. Hailey was just the vice president of the student government who had an idea for turning the paper into a digital edition.

It's easy enough to make those kinds of decisions when you're sitting alone in your room. It's a little harder when you're face-to-face with your "never-was-your-best-friend."

I was hoping that Michael would be waiting by my locker the next morning, but he wasn't. Hailey was. I was so surprised I honestly didn't know how to act.

"Sam," Hailey said in way she had never said my name before.

It sounded so cold and detached it hurt my heart.

"I heard Mrs. Brennan called you to her office," she continued stonily. "I just want you to know that I didn't rat on you. I heard that you thought I had. I wouldn't do that."

"Okay, thanks for letting me know," I said, trying to stop my voice from shaking. "And just so you know, I wouldn't tell anyone about your dyslexia, or make fun of it."

"So we're all good?" Hailey asked.

"All good," I agreed.

Hardly, I thought.

The rest of the day was just as tortuous as our brief conversation. I walked to classes with a group of other girls that I'm friends with, but every time I turned around, I'd see Hailey surrounded by her flock of Green Team admirers. The group seemed to be growing every minute. I was pretty sure that if they crowned a prom queen at this moment, Hailey would win by a landslide. She was superpopular. Everyone was talking about how great her ideas were and how lucky we were to have her on the student government. All hail Queen Hailey!

At lunchtime, I handed out some polls to random tables of students. I was in the middle of handing one to Michael Shea when Hailey tapped me on the shoulder.

"I thought we were all good," she said.

"That's what we said," I replied.

"So why are you trying to sabotage my subcommittee?" Hailey asked.

"What are you even talking about?" I asked.

"This!" Hailey said as she held up a poll paper in my face. "Why are you trying to make it seem like there are two choices here?"

"Um, maybe because there are?" I huffed. "You said I don't know how to see other people's point of view. Maybe you don't."

"Except that I do," Hailey snapped. "There are two choices when both of the choices are equal. There aren't two equal choices here. One is clearly the right thing to do. The other isn't."

"Says you," I said, sounding like I was five years old and fighting over crayons again.

"That is what I say," Hailey replied. "And as student government vice president, I'm not even sure it's within the rules to be handing out a poll in the cafeteria during school hours. I'm going to have to check into that."

"Please do," I said. "And I'll check with Mr. Trigg to make sure it's within the rules for the student government to interfere with

Cherry Valley Voice reporting."

Hailey tossed the poll on the floor and stormed off, her flock rushing behind her. She was definitely on a power trip. She thought she could stop me from handing out polls by intimidating me? Hardly.

Of course, who was witness to it all? Michael Lawrence. He was trying not to show his obvious amusement when he walked over to me.

"What's so funny now?" I said, still fuming.

"I just never realized how competitive you were," he said. "I mean, I know how competitive Hailey is because I've seen her on the soccer field. She's fierce. I just didn't know you were too."

"Me, fierce?" I snickered. "I thought I told you to give up the comedy act."

"Relax, Pasty," Michael said. "It was just an observation. I liked the way you stood up for the *Voice*. And I think a good article might help everyone see that there are more sides to this story— maybe even Hailey."

"I'm not so sure about that," I said.

"I know you're putting up a good front,"

Michael said. "But I also know how much you must miss her. I know how close you two are."

"Were," I corrected him.

"Are," he answered back. "If you didn't care about each other so much, you wouldn't be so mad right now."

I didn't have a snappy answer to that. He was right. It would be easy to just cut Hailey out of my life right now. I wish I didn't care. There was one big problem. I did care. Every time I looked at her, I wished things were the way they used to be. But every day it seemed like that ship was sailing farther away.

"Sam?" Michael said quietly. "I don't want you to be sad. I wish I could help fix this problem with Hailey."

"Thanks. I wish you could fix it too," I admitted.

"Well, I can't, but I did get a chance to do some research," Michael said. "Are you free Saturday afternoon? I have an early game, but I should be done by noon."

"Sure. Do you want to meet at the library?" I asked. "I'd invite you to my house, but my mom's really busy with work, and we're renovating and stuff."

"The library's perfect," Michael said. "One o'clock?"

"It's a date," I said. "Wait. I mean, you know, not a date, a meeting . . ."

Michael just ignored me and walked away. I'm pretty sure he was smiling.

Chapter 8

LOCAL LIBRARY SHOCKINGLY FILLED WITH PAPER!

★ ★ ★

On Saturday, I headed to the library. I was dressed a little nicer than if I were meeting just any friend at the library, but not so nice that it looked like I had taken the whole "date" thing seriously. Allie had helped with that. She had the casual but stylish look down cold, and she was really turning into quite the helpful sister these days. I'm guessing she must need something, or want me to hide something from Mom.

I had a stack of at least two hundred polls that I had collected at lunchtime the past couple of days, and I had a pile of research and opinion pieces on the benefits of reading the newspaper in print. I had even written down most of Mr. Trigg's soliloquy on the beauty of the printed page. We'd had a staff meeting for the *Voice* on Friday, and Mr. Trigg just went off on how much he loved paper. It was actually very cool but very unlike him. . . . It seemed like Trigg had thrown his reporter's tool kit out the window as he filled our newsroom with booming, poetic language—an ode to ink, and presses, and the long history of the newspaper, from the *Acta Diurna*, the first newspaper published in Rome, to the *Brooklyn Freeman* newspaper, published by the poet Walt Whitman, to the *Daily Mirror*, the first tabloid-style newspaper. I knew I wasn't alone in my passion for keeping the *Voice* in print, and Mr. Trigg let his true feelings spill out. We were all impressed and energized. There were a bunch of staffers who didn't think it was a bad idea to have the paper online, but everyone agreed we also wanted a print edition as well. I was curious to see what the polls would tell us.

I was organizing my notes when I noticed that it was already one fifteen. Michael wasn't usually late, so I sent him a text just to make sure I had gotten the time and place right. He texted back: *brt*.

Five minutes later, Michael stumbled into the library. He was still dressed in his baseball uniform, which was covered in dirt, and his hair looked damp with sweat. Not exactly your clean-cut "date" look, but I didn't mind—at all.

"I'm so sorry I'm late, Sam," he said, panting. "The game before us went into extra innings, so our game got pushed back, and then we went into extra innings, too, and then, well, here I am," he said as he tried to wipe some dirt off his cheek, but only smeared it around even more.

"And I thought I'd get to take a shower before our meeting," he apologized.

"As long as the librarian doesn't mind, it's okay by me," I said, pointing to the librarian, who was giving him the "SHHH!" sign.

The thing about Michael Lawrence's cuteness is that it is so powerful, it shines right through the dirt. In fact, he looked especially cute with his hair all tousled. The only problem was the smudge of mud on the tip of his nose—it was a little distracting. I kind of wanted to reach over and wipe it off myself, but I didn't know how he would feel about that. So I just swiped at my own nose a bit, and he got the hint.

"Well, did you at least win the game?" I laughed.

"Oh yeah, it was AWESOME!" Michael said, too loudly for the librarian, who was giving him the stink-eye again.

"Sorry," Michael whispered. "It was awesome. I was pitching a shutout, and so was the other team's pitcher. I was afraid that Coach would take me out when we went to extra innings, but we don't have another game until next Saturday, so he let me stay in. When I got up to bat at the bottom of the eleventh inning, we had a man on second. I hit a little blooper to right field, but their fielder couldn't get there in time and it was just enough for us to win the game."

"Congratulations!" I whispered back. "It sounds like it was exciting."

"It really was," Michael said. "Oh, and speaking of exciting, you should come to next week's game. I'm sure you'll find it thrilling."

"Why, are you planning to pitch another shut-out?" I asked.

"Always." Michael laughed. "But that's not what I meant. We're playing against West Hills. Your buddy Danny will be there. I'm sure he'd be happy to see you there."

"Then I'll definitely have to come," I replied. "Just to see you strike him out."

Michael put his hand on my head, rubbed my hair, looked right into my eyes, and smiled at me. If you didn't know any better, you might think it looked like the way you'd pet your dog, but it was so much better than that. It was like getting a note that said, "I'm glad that we're friends. I like talking to you; you're great," but with a gesture instead of words. Which was fine, because I knew I'd be able to replay that smile over and over in my mind later.

"I think we better to get to work," Michael said as he glanced at the librarian. "She does not look happy."

"I already started," I said, showing Michael my

piles. "I have some research about why reading a printed page is better. Did you know studies show that people read faster and strain their eyes less when they read paper? Also, it's not completely environmentally friendly to go digital. You have to use energy to read digital media, and that often comes from nonrenewable resources like coal, which are also contributing to global climate change."

"That's true, but you're still stopping the destruction of forests, and paper mills release waste material into the environment too," Michael countered. "I did some research too."

"You *did* research, or you just looked at the stuff Hailey gave you?" I asked.

"Whoa, why so defensive, Pasty?" Michael said. He looked a little surprised at me. "Of course I did some research of my own. We're supposed to be impartial, remember?"

He was right. We started to make a chart that listed the positive and negative features of both approaches. Surprisingly, it was pretty even in all columns. There wasn't a clear-cut "right way" like Hailey thought. But there wasn't a reason to not go digital either—unless you count a love of paper like Mr. Trigg and I would.

"We have some good stuff here," Michael noted. "It's definitely a strong foundation for our *unbiased* article. Let's look through the polls and see what everyone else thinks."

I had already created another chart with tally marks to record the poll responses from Buddybook, so we just went through the paper polls and added to it. Again, there wasn't a clear-cut answer. More kids said that they'd prefer the *Voice* to be printed digitally, but it was just a little more than half. And interestingly, about half the kids said they regularly read the paper but half said they would read it digitally if it were available.

"Another toss-up," I said. "What do you think?"

"I think we're journalists," Michael said. "We report the truth. We let other people use that information to make a decision."

"I'll report the truth," I replied. "But the truth is, I will be very upset if the decision is to stop printing the *Voice*."

Michael smiled, and not even the dirt could hide its brilliance.

"Believe it or not, Pasty, I will be too," he agreed. "I like seeing my name on a printed page. It's an ego thing, but I wouldn't admit it to anyone else."

"And in shocking Cherry Valley news, it's revealed that the star quarterback and pitcher of the championship baseball team has an ego." I laughed. "Who would have thought that?"

Michael leaned over and tugged on my hair again. This might be the best library visit ever!

"I think you should start writing the draft," Michael suggested. "Then I can go through it and make sure it's fair and balanced."

"What are you trying to say?" I asked.

"I'm not saying anything," he said. "But I think you'll agree that the Hailey situation has clouded your judgment just a little."

"I don't know about that," I said. "But I'll write the draft anyway."

"Speaking about the Hailey situation," Michael said. "How's that going?"

"It's great," I snarked. "I mean, having Mrs. Brennan think I'm some kind of horrible person and all."

"I thought Hailey told you she didn't say anything to Mrs. Brennan," said Michael.

"She did," I replied. "But . . . how would *you* know that?"

"I . . . um . . . I kind of heard . . . ," Michael stammered.

"The truth," I demanded.

"I've been talking to Hailey a little," Michael said.

"YOU WHAT?" I whisper yelled.

The librarian, who had been eyeing us the whole time, started to walk over to our table.

"She's really hurt, Sam," Michael explained. "I wish you would see that. She just needed someone to talk to."

"And *you're* that someone?" I asked. "She has a whole crowd of people surrounding her in school all the time. Why doesn't she talk to them?"

"I don't know, Sam," Michael admitted. "She called me. I think she just wanted to know if I knew how you felt. You know, it would be a lot easier if you just talked to her yourself."

"She *called* you?" I hissed. "And you told her how I felt?"

"Sam, I think you're blowing this out of proportion a little," Michael said. "It wasn't that big a deal. I know how close you guys were. I just wanted to help. You need to tell her how you feel."

"You can help by staying out of it," I replied, annoyed. "I'm going to go start the draft. I'll e-mail it to you, so you can make sure I'm *unbiased*."

I started to pack up all my stuff. I could feel that ball of emotions start to rise up in my throat again, and I wanted to get out of the library before Michael could see it too.

"Sam, I'm really sorry. I didn't mean to do anything wrong," Michael apologized.

"It's fine," I said, not meaning it at all. "I'll talk to you later."

I rushed out of the library before the librarian could get a chance to shush us. I could feel the tears streaming down my face as I walked home. How could such a great day be ruined? I really hated Hailey. I wanted to go home and think about how good it felt to be with Michael and how close we seemed to be getting. Now I was going to think about him and Hailey talking about *me*! I couldn't imagine what they said. Did they make fun of me? Was Michael on her side? Did Hailey tell him any of my secrets, like how I really felt about him? Well, besides blurting out that I had a crush on him. I mean, it was obviously not that big of a secret, and I'm sure he had a little hint that I really liked him, but still, that's different from having your best friend say it out loud. I would never do that to Hailey. I would never call a boy that she liked to talk about how mad I was at her. Although I wished I could right now.

At home, I couldn't stop thinking about everything that had happened. It felt like some awful movie, where the main character is betrayed by her best friend and shunned by everyone she knows. Was that where this was heading? Hailey would be the most popular girl at Cherry Valley Middle School, and I would be a total outcast? The more I thought about it, the more I cried, so

I took out the Dear Know-It-All letter, thinking I could at least try to write the column. Even I knew I'd have a hard time writing an impartial draft of the article right now. But when I started typing a reply to the grandma-sweater letter, other words came out of my fingertips:

Hailey,

I guess destroying the *Voice* wasn't enough for you. You had to hit me where it really hurts by calling my one true love, Michael Lawrence, and talking about me behind my back.

Guess what? You win. I wouldn't want to win that fight anyway, because I would never hurt anyone the way you hurt me.

—Sam

Just then, my door slammed open and Allie came waltzing in my room. I quickly reached for the hide screen key and turned around to block her view.

"Don't you ever knock?" I asked.

"Sorry, Sammy-pants. I thought we were cool," Allie said.

"STOP CALLING ME THAT!" I screamed. "And we are not cool if you think you can invade my privacy anytime you want."

"Do you have a problem?" Allie asked. "Is your little world torn apart because your BFF won't talk to you anymore? How tragic!"

It had been a long time since Allie and I had an actual physical fight. The last one I can remember was when I was six and was just learning how to roller skate. She put a stick on the sidewalk when I wasn't looking, so I tripped and fell. She said she didn't do it, but I'd seen the stick in her hand right before it happened, so when I got up and looked at my bleeding knees, I just lost it and charged at her, wheels and all.

I felt exactly the same way at that moment. All the anger I felt at Hailey, at Michael, at the world, at that moment, was directed right at my obnoxious big sister. I leaped out of my chair and charged at her. Allie knew it was coming, though, so she just grabbed my wrists and held me there.

"Calm down, Sam," she advised me. "I don't want to get into a fight with you. I just did my nails."

Mom came running up the stairs when she heard the commotion.

"What's going on here?" she asked.

"Sam lost it," Allie explained. "I just wanted to tell her about this great idea I had for redecorating her room, and she attacked me."

"Sam?" Mom said.

"I did lose it," I admitted. "But only because she was making fun of me. She thinks she's so great and she knows everything, but she doesn't know anything at all."

"I told you." Allie nodded to Mom. "Hormones."

I wanted to attack her again, but I knew I'd get in big trouble, so I just collapsed on my bed and put my pillow over my head.

"Leave me alone!" I cried. "I don't want either one of you in here."

"Let's go, Allie," Mom said. "Sam needs some space right now."

Chapter 9

CHERRY VALLEY REPORTER, LIKE THE CHEESE, STANDS ALONE

★ ★ ★

Mom was right, but she was also wrong. I needed some space so I could get control of myself for sure. On the other hand, the last thing I wanted was more space, because at the moment, the empty space was what was bothering me the most. I felt so alone in it.

I don't mind being by myself. I really don't. I like doing things that take only one person to do—like reading a book, or writing an article, or daydreaming—just fine. I *hated* this feeling of loneliness, though. Ever since the fight with Hailey, it was hanging over me like a cloud. Sure, it faded sometimes, like when Allie was being nice to me, or when I was spending time hanging out with Michael, or even talking to Mr. Trigg. It never really went away, though. It was like a black hole had sucked up all the happy space of our friendship. I had never really thought about it so much before—that happy space. It wasn't just the time that Hailey and I spent together that filled that space. It was the knowing—knowing there was always someone who would be there for me, someone I could call or text anytime and who would be sure to answer me, someone who would laugh at my stupid jokes, or tell me my new hairstyle looked great, even when it didn't, but then help me fix it. Not having that knowing, and being aware that what was left behind was the polar opposite of knowing—someone who was talking about me behind my back, someone who probably was laughing about me with her new friends—that was the worst of it.

I spent a week letting that cloud completely cover me. Mom and Allie tried to be extra nice to me, but I just moped around the house. Michael made sure to wave or smile at me at least once every day in school, but I just waved back and went on to my next class. I e-mailed him my draft and didn't have the energy to come up with a cute note to send with it. Even Mr. Trigg tried to cheer me up by doing a hilariously bad Churchill impression, and at any other time I would have cracked up, but I just forced the edges of my mouth to turn up into a fake smile.

I couldn't stand to even go near the cafeteria. On Monday, I thought I would just go grab a quick bite by myself when I saw Michael and Hailey standing in line chatting with each other. It made my stomach turn, and I didn't feel hungry anymore. I got a lot of homework and studying done in the library during lunch period that week. It was the only place I knew I'd be safe.

Friday nights were usually Hailey's and my sleepover night. I wondered if Hailey was having another friend sleep over—maybe even a few of them, since it seemed like she had so many now. I decided to finish cleaning out my room, and it was a lot easier now. I didn't really want to keep anything anymore. My Maybe box was still in Allie's room, but almost everything else went into the trash—everything but the jump rope that Hailey had given me. I cried when I found it stuffed in the back of one of my dresser drawers. That was how Hailey and I had first started talking to each other. She was jumping rope at recess in kindergarten, and I just sat there and watched, because I didn't know how to do it. She asked me if I wanted to try and waited while I clumsily attempted. She wasn't like the other kids, who didn't want to share, or who would have gotten annoyed that it was taking me so long to learn. She just sat there and kept giving me tips and pointers, and the next day Hailey gave me a present after school—a jump rope of my very own. She had told her mom about me and asked if they could get me one. It was the best present I had ever gotten—a best friend.

As much as the angry side of me wanted to throw the jump rope away, I just couldn't. It would mean throwing our friendship in the trash too. And even though it felt like it already was, there was little piece inside of me that hoped it wasn't.

I carried four trash bags out of my room, and

it looked incredibly neat and clean—and more
depressing than ever. I turned on my computer and
decided to finish the Dear Know-It-All column.

Dear Tight Fit,

I think you should move on. If you don't know
someone who would like the sweater, like a little
sister or a cousin, you could donate it. There
are a lot of organizations that accept old
clothes. Sometimes even the best things have
to end, like the feeling you get when you put on
a comfortable sweater. That's just life.

-Dear Know-It-All

I saved the document and turned off the computer, then fell asleep with the jump rope under
my pillow. The next morning, I woke up when I
heard a knock on my door.

"Come in," I growled sleepily.

"Morning, Sam," Allie said with cheerleader
perkiness. "Time to rise and shine!"

I wasn't sure what was going on, maybe hormones? Allie had hardly spoken to me since I
charged at her. Or maybe she had and I'd just

ignored it. I wasn't exactly sure. Allie bustled around my room, shuffling through my closet, opening and closing drawers in my dresser. She placed an outfit at the foot of my bed.

"Get in the shower, Sam," Allie commanded. "Then get dressed and come eat breakfast."

"And I am following your orders because . . . ?" I wondered.

"Oh, come on, Sam. What else are you going to do?" Allie said. "Mope around all day? Mom's going to take us somewhere in a little while."

"Is it for our rooms?" I asked.

"Something like that," Allie replied. "And hurry. Mom made homemade waffles, and you know how rare that is!"

"Did she finish her big project?" I asked, confused.

"No, still another week to go," Allie said. "But she's in the homestretch."

I mechanically carried the outfit to the bathroom and turned on the faucet. The warm water washed away the saltiness that my dried tears had left behind. I could taste it as the water ran down my face. The outfit was once again a masterpiece of casual but cute, and I had to admit that I even felt a little better after I put it on.

The good feelings continued as I shoved Mom's waffles into my mouth. I realized that I had hardly been eating all week, and that was totally unlike me. I usually can't get enough to eat.

"So where are we going today?" I mumbled, syrup dripping from my lips. "Paint store? Furniture shopping?"

"Samantha, please wait until you finish chewing," Mom said, but she was laughing. "Although I'm so happy to see you eating again, I'll make an exception."

"I'm happy to see you eating with us again," I said, gulping down my waffle. "And that the end of your big accounting project is in sight!"

"Yes, let's toast the end of Mom's project!" Allie said, raising her glass of orange juice.

We clinked our OJ glasses together, and Mom even did a "Woop-woop!"

After breakfast, we cleaned up together and headed out. Allie and I raced to the car to get dibs on the front seat. Allie won, but she let me sit in the front anyway. I was starting to get a little suspicious. Allie never gives up the front seat without an argument.

I was even more suspicious when Mom started heading in the direction of school and not toward the mall.

"Where are we going, Mom?" I asked.

"Don't worry, honey," Mom answered. "We'll get there soon enough."

"There" was good old Cherry Valley Middle School, and Mr. Trigg was standing at the side of the parking lot, waving us into a spot. Now I wasn't just suspicious. I was totally confused.

"Mom, can you please explain?" I said.

"Sure, Sam. It's not that complicated," Mom said. "Mr. Trigg told me that there was a baseball game this morning, and he wanted to brush up on his knowledge of the sport, so we thought you might join him."

"You know, because he's used to cricket," Allie said.

"You guys, that is so lame." I sighed. "Is this

your attempt to get me out of the house?"

"Guilty," Mom said. "Don't be mad."

"I'm not," I said. "I know I've been tough to live with lately. And, Allie, just for your information, it's *not* hormones. But I am sorry for the way I acted."

"Apology accepted," Allie said. "Just try to have some fun today, okay?"

"I'll try, but I can't promise," I said as I got out of the car. "I mean, it's a Saturday and I'm going to a baseball game with a teacher!"

"Cheerio!" Mom called, driving off.

I rolled my eyes. Mom could be so corny sometimes.

"Cheerio!" Mr. Trigg called back to her.

I guess it takes one to know one.

"Miss Martone, are you ready to show me the intricacies of America's pastime?" Mr. Trigg asked as we walked to the bleachers.

"Mr. Trigg, I believe you might know them better than I do." I laughed. "But I'll try."

Mr. Trigg walked right past the home section of the bleachers and sat down in the visitor's section.

"Okay, first thing is, you're sitting in the wrong place," I said. "This is for the fans of the other team."

"I'm aware of that, Samantha," Mr. Trigg said. "As a journalist, I'd rather see what the other side thinks. I already know how our fans feel."

"Interesting approach," I noted. "I never thought of it before."

I was particularly happy that Mr. Trigg had chosen our spot when I saw Hailey sitting in the stands with her soccer teammates. At least it wasn't her Green Team minions, I thought.

The teams ran onto the field for warm-ups. I saw Michael look around the bleachers and wondered if he was looking for me. Then I saw Hailey wave to him and figured he wasn't. I was watching them closely when I heard someone shouting my name.

"Hey, Sam!" Danny Stratham said, trotting over to the bleachers. "I see you're sitting in the winner's section. Smart girl."

I couldn't help but laugh. He wasn't as cute as Michael, but there was something about his breezy, flirty mannerisms that made him incredibly easy to talk to. Of course, it seemed like every other girl in West Hills *and* Cherry Valley felt that way. I could practically feel some of the eye daggers the West Hills girls were throwing my way.

"What's up, Danny?" I called back. "I'm just sitting here as an impartial observer."

"Well, you won't be impartial for long," Danny replied. "Once you see me play, you won't want anyone else to win."

"I don't know about that," I teased. "I have the head of an unbiased reporter, but my heart is with Cherry Valley."

"Hearts can change," Danny called as he ran back into his position on the field.

I looked over and saw that both Hailey and Michael were staring at me. Ugh! Hopefully Michael knew that it was all in good fun. But looking at the scrunched-up expression on his face, I had a feeling he didn't.

It turned out that Mr. Trigg and I did seem to be sitting on the winning side, as West Hills got off a quick lead. Michael was pitching, but he definitely seemed off his game. I wondered if his arm still hadn't recovered from the extra-inning shutout he had pitched last week.

In the first inning there were West Hills players on second and third with one out when Danny Stratham approached the plate. I cringed when he turned and pointed his bat at me. I wanted to melt into my seat when he hit the first pitch over the fence. West Hills 3, Cherry Valley 0.

"That was quite an impressive shot your friend hit," Mr. Trigg observed.

"He's not really my friend," I corrected him. "Just an acquaintance. But I agree; it was impressive."

The next three innings didn't go much better. Michael really struggled on the mound, and it seemed like he couldn't find the strike zone, as much as he tried. Danny continued to show off, making an incredible catch of a hard-hit line drive to end the third inning. I was worried he was going to toss the ball to me, but luckily he saved me from that embarrassment.

"I think I'm ready for a snack now," I said to

Mr. Trigg. "Would you like anything?"

"Thank you, Samantha, but I had a rather filling breakfast, so I'll pass on the refreshments for the time being," replied Mr. Trigg.

"I had a big breakfast, too, but I think it just made me hungrier." I laughed.

I headed to the refreshment stand to grab a hot pretzel and a sports drink. I felt a little uncomfortable because all of the kids and parents on the Cherry Valley side were looking at me like I was a traitor, especially the girls from Hailey's soccer team. I wish I could have been wearing a badge that said, "Impartial reporter, just trying to gather information about the other side." I even thought about whispering it to one person and telling them to pass it around. I figured if things kept going the way they were going for Cherry Valley, Mr. Trigg and I were going to have to find new seats soon.

I got my snacks—plural, because I couldn't resist grabbing a pack of red licorice—and started to climb back up the bleachers when I heard Danny Stratham calling my name again.

This time, he was on the field. Actually, he was up at bat again, and he stopped the game to call my name. I tried to ignore him and continued climbing, but he just kept shouting my name even louder.

"Sam! Watch this!" Danny called while every Cherry Valley fan glared at me.

I turned around, hoping he would stop, and watched as he hit the ball right past the pitcher. Michael nearly caught it as it grazed right past his glove, but he didn't, and Danny ran to first safely.

I tried to slink back to my seat, but stumbled and spilled my drink all over myself. A bunch of people on the Cherry Valley side laughed, and Hailey's friends hooted and hollered like it was the funniest thing they had ever seen. I saw Hailey put her hands over her face. I guess she thought it was hysterical too.

I didn't see the rest of the game. I was covered with blue drink, which was probably appropriate, because it matched the way I felt—blue. I went to my seat and explained to Mr. Trigg that I needed to go home and change. He understood and offered me a ride home, but I needed to walk off the embarrassment. I told him to enjoy the rest of the game; then I texted Mom to let her know I was on the way. I crept back down the bleachers and left the field, feeling as alone as I had all week.

Mom met me at the door. Somehow she was acting even more suspiciously than she had earlier. She was holding a new shirt in her hand.

"I'm sorry you didn't have a great time," she said. "I was really hoping you would."

"It's okay," I said. "What's with the shirt?"

"Oh, Mr. Trigg called and told me about your accident," she said. "He said you needed to change."

"I do," I said. "But I can go upstairs and do that."

"Oh no, don't," Mom said, opening the door to her office. "Just change in here. I thought we could run out and get some ice cream."

"I don't really feel like having another snack," I said. "And why can't I go upstairs?"

"Okay, I'll confess," Mom said. "Allie and I

started working on your room. She had a great idea and wanted to surprise you. I think you'll really like it."

"Allie's doing *my room*!" I cried. "What if I hate it?"

"If you do, we'll do it over," Mom said. "Just let her try, Sam. It really means a lot to her."

"Fine." I huffed. "But don't think I will not call a do over. And now you owe me a triple-scoop cone."

"You got it," Mom said as she grabbed her car keys. "Now change your shirt and meet me in the car."

Chapter 10

BIG SISTER FOR THE WIN!

★ ★ ★

I'm sure you're wondering how I could control myself and not rush up the stairs to see what Allie was doing to my room. If it had happened at any other time, that's probably exactly what I would do. But I was tired of fighting, and tired of being upset, so I thought it would be easier to just give in and let Mom buy me ice cream. I knew that whatever Allie did would look good, because it always does. I was pretty sure it wouldn't be "me," though.

I was 100 percent, absolutely, positively sure I was going to return and find my room bright and colorful and "sparkling with pizzazz," and that even if it didn't need a complete do over, I was going to have a lot of work to do to tone it down a few notches.

Mom stalled as much as she could. After ice cream, we stopped at the mall; then we went to the office supply store to pick up some ink and printing paper, and then finally we returned home. Allie was sitting at the kitchen counter, trying to look calm and cool, but I could tell she was really excited. I didn't think I had it in me to hide how I would really feel.

"Close your eyes, Sam," Allie said as she grabbed my hand.

She led me up the stairs, and we stopped at the entrance to my room.

"Okay, you can look now," she said, clapping her hands with delight before I could even sneak a peek.

I actually gasped when I opened my eyes. It couldn't have been more perfect if Allie had snuck into my brain and pulled out a vision of my perfect room.

Three of the walls were painted a grayish lavender. It was subtle; it was pretty; it was so, so me. Allie had stenciled words on the walls: "Dream" and "Write" and "Create." The most shocking part was the fourth wall. It was my Maybe box. Allie had turned the whole wall into a collage with every scrap of paper, every movie ticket, every memory that was in the box. For the hundredth time that week, my eyes filled up with tears.

"You hate it," Allie said. "I'm really sorry."

I grabbed Allie and hugged her so tightly it hurt. I couldn't stop crying, but I didn't want to.

"It's perfect," I whispered.

I lifted my head and saw that Allie was smiling, but Mom was crying too.

"I thought it would be," Allie said. "I love you, Sam. Even though we argue, even though we fight, ever though we're probably as different as two sisters can be—I love you, okay? Always remember that. And I know that you've been going through some tough stuff lately, so I just wanted to make you happy."

I smiled at her, and this time I didn't have to force the edges of my mouth up. It was a real smile.

"I love it," I said. "And I love you, too. You're amazing."

"Group hug," Mom said, putting her arms around us.

The three of us stood there laughing and hugging and crying.

"It's not finished yet," Allie said. "We need to pick up some new furniture and accessorize and stuff, but I had this idea when I was going through your box and I wanted to surprise you."

"I'm surprised." I laughed. "But if you don't mind, there's something I need to do."

"Are you going to call Hailey?" Allie asked. "Because I don't want to tell you what to do, but I do think you should."

"No, I'm not," I answered. "Not now, anyway."

Mom and Allie went downstairs and I sat in the middle of my room for a minute, just to take it all in. I couldn't wait to go to sleep that night, just so I could wake up and see it all again.

I turned on my computer and reopened the Dear Know-It-All document. I knew my first answer needed a revision.

Dear Tight Fit,

I don't think you have to move on, but you can move forward. If you're happy wearing the sweater, then I say don't worry about what anyone thinks. But if you outgrow it, you could always turn the sweater into something else, like a big bag you can carry your stuff in, or mittens and a hat, or a throw pillow for your bed. This way you can keep it close to you all the time, just in a different way.

-Dear Know-It-All

★　★　★

On Monday morning, I got to school early so I could stop by Mr. Trigg's office and apologize for leaving the game early. I handed in the Dear Know-It-All column and told him I had e-mailed my article draft to Michael and was waiting for his revision. I hadn't heard a peep from him since the game.

I almost tripped over him in the hallway, though, but he ignored me and kept going. I could tell he was really upset, probably because he thought I was cheering for West Hills—and Danny Stratham. What was that advice you gave me about sharing your feelings, Michael Lawrence? I figured he needed a reminder, so I waited by his locker at the end of the school day.

He almost turned around and walked the other

way after he saw me standing there, but then I could tell he realized how dumb that would look. I mean, it was *his* locker.

"Excuse me, Sam," Michael said as he plopped his backpack on the floor.

"I know you're upset," I said. "I just wanted to explain."

"Who said I'm upset?" Michael asked.

"No one said it, although you should," I replied.

"Why should I?" questioned Michael.

"Because you're not following your own advice," I informed him. "You told me that I should just say how I'm feeling. But you're not. So I'm going to tell you what happened, and you're going to listen. And then if you're still upset, fine."

I explained why Mr. Trigg and I were sitting on the West Hills side of the bleachers and that I didn't know why Danny acted like that to me, but probably a big factor was that he knew it bothered Michael, and that I left because I had spilled a drink all over myself and was embarrassed and I was upset that Hailey had laughed at me, not because of any other reason. I could see Michael listening closely, and I could tell he was feeling better about the whole situation.

"Well, thanks for explaining about the bleachers, because that did really upset me," Michael admitted. "I can see Mr. Trigg's point, but next time you come to my game, you better be a fan and not a reporter."

"I promise," I replied.

"And, Sam, honestly, if you like Danny Stratham, I understand," he said. "A lot of girls do. He's a pretty popular guy."

"I think I told you this before, but I guess I need to repeat it," I answered. "I do like Danny Stratham. He's funny and he's easy to talk to. But he can also be kind of a jerk. He's not my friend. You are. And I don't feel the same way about him as I do about you at all."

Then I stopped. I figured that was a kind of subtle way to let Michael know that even though I considered him a friend, the way I felt about him was a little deeper than that, without having to embarrass myself and say it outright. Or at least I hoped it was subtle.

"You didn't have to tell me that," Michael said. "But it does make me feel better."

He reached over and rumpled my hair again, and I knew that things were going to be back to normal for the best reporting duo Cherry Valley had ever seen. *One down, one to go*, I thought. Unfortunately, the one that was left was the really tough one.

Chapter 11

THE GREEN TEAM FACES OFF WITH THE *VOICE*

★ ★ ★

On Tuesday, Michael and I met after school to work on the final version of our Green Team article. He had a done a really good job revising it, and I could see it was a lot more balanced than my first draft had been. We proofread it one last time.

"I guess it's all set for Trigg," I said.

"Maybe not," Michael replied. "I had an idea."

Michael explained that he thought we should present our research at the next student government meeting and propose a compromise. Then we'd have a real ending to our story. It was a good plan, even if it meant facing Hailey.

We sat in the front row of the auditorium

at Wednesday's student government meeting. Mr. Trigg and the rest of the *Voice* staff joined us. Michael had already talked to Anthony about speaking, and Anthony called us up to the podium. We took turns presenting all our findings, summing up the information in our pro-versus-con chart.

"In conclusion," I said, "we'd like to propose a compromise. We will publish a digital edition of the *Cherry Valley Voice*. We'd also like to continue to print a paper edition, but we'll print fewer copies, so that only the students who really want a printed copy will get one. We'll also look into printing on recycled paper. Even though it costs a little more money, we can publicize the fact that we are 'going green,' and maybe other newspapers will take notice. Mr. Trigg will help us with that."

Michael and I went back to our seats, and Anthony returned to the podium.

"I think that Michael Lawrence and Samantha Martone have come up with an excellent compromise," Anthony said. "My vote is in favor of it. Does anyone have any objections?"

I could see that Hailey was about to raise her hand, but she didn't. I wondered why.

"Since there are no objections, the GO GO subcommittee will now work to help the *Cherry Valley Voice* publish both a print and a digital edition and will help the staff find good sources for environmentally friendly printing options," Anthony concluded.

Hailey immediately got up, came over to Michael and me, and held out her hand.

"Congratulations," she said coldly. "I hope a pile of paper was worth destroying our friendship over."

Then she rushed out of the auditorium.

I was stunned. It would have hurt less if she had punched me.

"Ouch," Michael said.

"*I* destroyed our friendship?" I gasped. "What is she talking about? She's the one who came up with this whole GO GO idea."

"You know, someone once gave me some very good advice," Michael said.

"Let me guess. . . . I should tell her how I really feel." I laughed.

"Great advice," Michael noted. "Whoever came up with that should think about being a guidance counselor."

I reached up and rumpled his hair the way he usually did to mine.

"Can you finish the article?" I called as I rushed down the aisle. "I'm going to be a little busy."

I knew which way Hailey walked home, so I ran until I saw her up ahead.

"Hailey!" I yelled when I was close enough for her to hear me.

She didn't stop walking.

"Hailey!" I yelled again.

She still didn't stop.

I caught up to her and walked by her side, but she wouldn't even turn to look at me.

"Hailey," I said. "I just wanted to explain how I've been feeling."

"I think you already did that pretty clearly," Hailey replied.

"Huh?" I said, confused. "When did I do that?"

"Guess what? You win," Hailey said, trying to imitate my voice.

That's when it hit me. Hailey had gotten the e-mail that I'd written just to get my feelings off my chest, not to send her! I must have hit the send key instead of hide screen when Allie had barged into my room.

"I don't think you need to say anything more," Hailey added. "You've said enough. And guess what? You did win. So just leave me alone."

I really didn't know what to say to her then. I had a whole bunch of feelings inside of me, and I wanted to get them out, but I also didn't want to say anything without thinking about it first. Because obviously that strategy wasn't very effective. So I just went with the only thing I could think of at the moment.

"I'm sorry," I said.

Then I turned around and headed home, alone again.

★   ★   ★

The rest of the week flew by. The newsroom was a flurry of activity as everyone was excited about the new digital publishing plan. Mr. Trigg invited some computer designers from the local paper to come in to show us some tricks. We had launched a digital version of the *Voice* a while back, but it was really basic. The computer designers gave us some tips on how to make our newspaper look really professional and great on-screen.

At home, the decorating committee was in full swing, and my room was looking even more amazing by the minute. Oh, and the sparkling with pizzazz design? Totally the new look for Allie's room.

I was still searching for a way to solve the whole Hailey dilemma, though. I was past the point of being angry. I just wanted to find a way to put it all behind me so we could move on, whether we would ever be best friends again or not. It was so uncomfortable seeing each other around school. Now I knew that every time Hailey looked at me—even when she was surrounded by her friends—the look that she was giving me wasn't spiteful. She seemed as upset as I was, and I really felt terrible about sending the e-mail. I had hurt my best friend as much as she had hurt me, and I didn't know how to make it better.

I even told Michael all about the e-mail. Considering that we were calling ourselves friends now, and not just co-reporters, and considering that he had already cared enough to try to make things better between us, I thought he might have some more advice for me. He was stumped, though.

"That's tough, Sam," he said. We were at his house hanging out. "Did you tell her that you didn't mean to send it?"

"I didn't get a chance," I said. "And that would just sound stupid anyway. I wrote it, so obviously I felt that way. Whether I sent it or not doesn't really matter."

"That's true," he said. "I still think you both just need to tell each other how you feel."

"That's a little hard to do when the other person won't listen," I said. "Not that I blame her."

"I'm sure you'll figure out it," Michael said. "And if you need my help, I'll be there."

"I know," I said. "I do have one favor to ask you."

"Sure. What do you need?" Michael asked.

"Could you pitch a little better the next time you play West Hills?" I joked. "Maybe even strike out Danny Stratham?"

"Oh, that is a definite yes," Michael replied.

"Good," I said. "Maybe a fastball or something." I was totally joking around. I don't really know the difference between a fastball and a curveball.

"Well, aren't you Little Miss Know-It-All herself?" said Michael, laughing.

I stopped laughing. "Why would you say that?" I panicked. No one was supposed to know I was Dear Know-It-All.

"Wait . . . what?" said Michael. "I was just joking."

"You said I was Know-It-All!" I said, my face getting hot.

"Well . . . ," said Michael, looking straight at me. "Aren't you?"

"No," I said quickly. "Nope. Not me. Not at all. I mean, I never really know anything about anything. How could I know anything to write about?

Or tell people what to do? I'm a mess."

Michael was smiling at me. "Okay," he said. "You are Dear Know-Nothing."

"Yep!" I said. "That's me!" I was trying to figure out if Michael believed me or if he was just teasing me. I was kind of tired from all the drama of the past few weeks. I didn't want to guess anymore.

"I don't like Danny Stratham," I said.

"You said that," said Michael.

"I like you," I said. Oh. My. God. Did I just say that? Did aliens come down and abduct my mouth?

"I like you too, Sam," said Michael. He was smiling a lot now.

We sat there looking at each other for a while.

"Okay, well, I should get going," I said. "I told my mother I would be home by now."

"I'll walk you halfway," said Michael.

I wondered if he noticed that I was walking really slowly. It was just kind of nice to be walking together, not saying anything.

"Well, this is halfway," he said. We stopped.

He reached over and whispered in my ear, "I like you a lot, Sam." Six little words. Six shocking words. I was so surprised I kind of whipped my head around, and when I did, his mouth landed on mine, and well . . . we kind of stayed there for a second. I don't think he meant to kiss me. We were both a little startled. But neither of us really pulled away either. It. Was. Awesome. And at that moment, there was only one person I wanted to tell all about it.

Chapter 12

BREAKING NEWS: THERE ARE SOME THINGS YOU NEVER OUTGROW

★ ★ ★

Allie came into my room on Saturday morning carrying a big package. It was a new comforter and sheet set for my bed, with inspirational words printed all over it. Perfect, of course.

"Did you ever work things out with Hailey?" Allie asked.

"Nope," I said. "I really don't know how to."

Allie and I stripped the sheets off my bed. She held up the jump rope that was still under my pillow.

"What's this?" she asked. "It seems like it would be a little uncomfortable to sleep on. Is it part of that new sleep routine?"

"No." I laughed. "It's just a reminder."

I told Allie the story of the jump rope and how Hailey and I first became friends. It seemed like something that everyone should have known already, but I guess if you weren't there, how would you know?

"I think that's your clue," Allie said, holding up the jump rope.

"It is?" I asked.

"Yep," said Allie. "You need to think about the reasons that you and Hailey first became friends, and you need to remind her of that."

"Did I ever tell you you're amazing?" I asked.

"Maybe once." Allie laughed. "But keep saying it."

Allie had given me the seed for the perfect plan. I worked late into the night, a lot later than my sleep routine usually allowed, but on Sunday morning, I was all ready.

I hit the print key on my computer, threw the paper in my backpack, and grabbed the jump rope.

"Where are you going with that?" Mom asked as I headed out the door. "I haven't seen you use that thing in years."

"I haven't," I said. "It's just like riding a bicycle—something you never forget how to do. Oh, and I'm just running to Hailey's for a little bit. Is that okay?"

"It's more than okay," Mom replied, smiling. "Good luck!"

I knew Hailey would be driving home with her family soon. They always had Sunday breakfast at the diner together, and I knew I was about to totally humiliate myself in front of them, but it didn't matter. Some things are a lot more important.

I planted myself on Hailey's front lawn and attempted to jump rope. At first, I was as pathetic as the first time I tried to do it in the school yard. But it is like bike riding, something that sticks in your muscle memory, I guess. I jumped up and down and sang our favorite jump rope songs at the top of my lungs, just like I was little again.

Hailey's mom and dad pulled up and waved to me. I knew they probably thought I was crazy, but I also knew that like my mom, they knew how much this fight was hurting Hailey—and me. After the rest of her family went inside, Hailey stood at the car and stared at me. I didn't care. I kept on jumping.

"What are you doing, Sam?" Hailey asked. "You're embarrassing yourself. You are really terrible at jumping rope. And we're totally too old to be doing that."

"I don't care," I said.

I kept on singing:

"Strawberry shortcake
Huckleberry pie
Who's going to be your lucky guy?
A, B, C . . ."

"That's not how it goes, Sam," Hailey said.

"Oh yeah?" I replied. "Then show me."

I handed the jump rope to Hailey. She started jumping like an expert, of course.

"Strawberry shortcake
Cream on top
Tell me the name of your sweetheart.
Is it A, B, C . . . ?"

"That's how it goes," Hailey said after she jumped all the way to *Z*.

"Now I remember," I said. "Do you remember

when you gave me this jump rope?"

Hailey started to cry. "I'm sorry, Sam," she said. "I can't."

"Hailey, please," I said, starting to cry too. "Just give me five minutes. After all the jump roping we've shared, could you just give me five minutes?"

It was working. Hailey put her head down, but didn't leave. I picked up my backpack and took out the paper. I didn't show her yet, but it was a four-page newspaper. I had spent all night writing and designing it. The headline on the front page read: *Cherry Valley Rejoices as BFFs Reunite*.

There was no story under the headline, though.

"I just want to show you something," I said as I sat down on her front steps. "I made it for you."

I handed the newspaper to Hailey. She started to cry more when she read the headline.

"I actually did it a little backward," I said. "The front page is the latest news. The story starts inside."

I opened up the paper and pointed to the article

on the top left. It was titled: *Girl Takes Friend Under Her Wing in School Yard*.

I had found a picture of Hailey and me jumping rope when we were little. Even though it wasn't taken in the school yard, it fit the story perfectly. I wrote all about that day at recess. Every other article on the page was a story from our friendship. *Martone Visits Best Friend in Hospital After Tonsillectomy; Hailey and Sam Head Off to Middle School; Hailey Victorious in Student Government Election*.

The last page was taken up by one story.

Best Friends Fight; Observers Fear They Will Never Make Up.

I wrote every single thing that happened in that story, from when I started feeling like Hailey had abandoned me to the moment when I knew that Hailey had mistakenly gotten my e-mail. I tried to be a good reporter and write a fair and balanced account. I really hoped that I had succeeded.

Hailey stopped crying as she read all the stories. When she got to the end of the last page, she looked up at me.

"I can't believe you did all of this," she said.

"That's what friends do," I replied. "Hailey, I don't know what to say besides I'm sorry," I continued. "I really thought you were trying to hurt me. And I just kept getting angrier and angrier about it. I should have told you how I felt from the beginning, but it always seemed like you were too busy to talk to me."

"I thought you were trying to hurt *me*," Hailey said. "I thought you would be so excited about a digital edition—it's the way almost every newspaper is heading, so I thought it would give you a great start for your journalism career. I was so excited to announce it and I was so proud of the GO GO name. I thought you'd love it. I never thought you'd be mad about it."

"Well, I was," I said. "I guess I thought you knew me better. Anyway, we obviously have a lot to work out," I added. "That's why I left the front page blank. I was hoping that even if you can't be my best friend again, we can at least figure out a way to be nice to each other."

"Um . . . why can't we be best friends again?" Hailey asked.

There were so many things I wanted to say when Hailey said that, but none of them could really express the way I was feeling. So I just put my head on her shoulder and cried. I felt Hailey's head rest on mine, and our tears mixed together and splattered on the front page. It was like they were writing the cover story.

"Hey, did you know that Allie redecorated my room?" I sniffed.

"Are you kidding me?" Hailey said. "I have *got* to see that. Is it gold and bright pink?"

"Why don't you come over?" I suggested. "It's actually pretty amazing."

"I'd like to," Hailey said.

I handed the newspaper to Hailey and she ran inside to put it away and to tell her parents that she was going to my house for a bit. She came out with her old jump rope in her hand.

I'm sure that if anyone from Cherry Valley Middle School saw us skipping down the street singing jump rope songs, they would have wondered what was wrong with us. They probably would have said something like, "Look at those two girls skipping rope down the street! They are too old to be doing something as silly as that." We didn't care. We had each other. Nothing else mattered. That's what friends are for.

IF YOU ENJOYED THE DEAR KNOW-IT-ALL BOOKS, CHECK OUT THIS NEW SIMON SPOTLIGHT SERIES:

IT TAKES TWO

A Whole New Ball Game

by Belle Payton

1

CHAPTER ONE

"It's soooo hot in Texas!"

"It's soooo hot in Texas!"

Alex and Ava Sackett blurted out the same words at the same time. They did this a lot. Their mom always said it was a twin thing.

"If someone handed me a pair of scissors right now, I'd chop off my entire ponytail," said Ava.

"Then I suppose it's a good thing the scissors are still packed in a box somewhere," sighed their mother.

Alex rolled her eyes. "Must you always speak in such hyperbole, Ava?" She bumped her sister over a fraction of an inch. "Don't hog the fan. And don't even kid about chopping off your perfect, gorgeous curls!"

The two girls were sitting on the floor,

sprawled against the wall of their new living room, sharing a single, not-very-large fan.

"Who's kidding?" Ava replied, bumping her sister back. "*You* have perfect, gorgeous curls. My hair is just a giant pain."

"What are you talking about?" Alex asked indignantly. "We have the exact same hair!"

As she spoke, Alex patted her own hair as if to make sure it was still there. It was, of course—piled into a topknot that was both stylish and practical in the scorching heat. Ava's chocolate-brown curls, on the other hand, were gathered into a messy ponytail. Loose strands had escaped and were plastered to her neck, making her even hotter. Ava couldn't help but notice that Alex's hair had stayed put on top of her head and wasn't stuck to her neck.

"Girls, it's too hot to bicker," said Mrs. Sackett. She'd given up trying to unpack the kitchen and was splayed in the one chair not stacked with boxes and other junk. She lifted the already-melting, ice-filled bag from the top of her head and applied it to the sides of her neck, like she was dabbing herself with perfume. "I'm sure your father will have the AC up and running any minute now."

From the office, Alex and Ava's older brother, Tommy, let loose a triumphant cry. He appeared in the doorway holding a second fan above his head, like a wide receiver who'd just scored the winning touchdown. "Found it!" he said, shoving a box out of the way to plug it in. He, too, slumped to the floor to bask in the flowing air, which rippled his own brown curls.

Ava got tired of jockeying for space in front of the fan. She stood up and drifted lazily over to the window, which looked out over the backyard. Beyond the fence was the back-yard of the house on the next block in their development, and beyond that, a vast, treeless landscape, flat as an ocean, all browns, grays, and gray-greens. The colors in Texas were very different from the lush darker greens of their backyard outside of Boston.

Across the room she could see through the doorway into the kitchen, where their Australian shepherd, Moxy, lay on her side, panting. The kitchen floor was probably the coolest surface in the house, but that wasn't saying much. Moxy looked at Ava, the whites of her eyes visible as she gazed upward, as if asking Ava to explain what on earth had happened to the Sackett family. One day they were in Massachusetts, with a backyard full of squirrels to chase and lavish garden beds to dig up, and the next they were in dry, barren Texas, where it was too hot for any self-respecting dog to even *consider* chasing after a squirrel.

Suddenly there was a groan and a whir and then a *whoosh*, and the air conditioner started up. All four of them cheered. Almost immediately, cool air began flowing through the house.

"Thank goodness," said their mom.

"Here comes Daddy," said Alex, as they heard footsteps bounding through the kitchen.

Coach Mike Sackett stepped over Moxy and joined his family in the living room. The air-conditioner repairman followed behind him.

"Much appreciated, Bill," said their father to the repairman, shaking his hand.

Bill saluted. "No problem, Coach," he said. "I'm sure y'all will get used to the Texas heat eventually. Must be quite a change from where you folks came from."

Coach nodded. "We'll get used to it, and everything else," he said, leading the man toward the front door.

"Practice start tomorrow?" Bill asked.

"Yes sir, it sure does."

"Team look okay?"

Coach chuckled. "We're young. It's going to be a rebuilding year, but I have high hopes for the boys," he said.

Bill hovered in the doorway, not yet ready to leave. "So what's your strategy against Culver City, Coach? I was talking to some of the guys at the shop, and they were saying Culver's got more size this year. You'll probably want to spread the field, right?"

Coach patted him on the back and guided him out the front door. "That makes sense. I appreciate the perspective," he said, and waved the man out.

"Another football fan!" said Mrs. Sackett with a little laugh as Coach shut the door. "There seem to be a lot of them in Ashland!"

Coach grinned. "It's just the culture," he said. "Lots of die-hard football types. It was the same way when I was growing up around here. Everyone in Ashland pays attention to the Ashland Tigers. It's a nice, close-knit community, Laur. You'll see. I'm going to watch some film."

"Ooh! What film are you going to watch, Daddy? Can I watch with you?" asked Alex, who had paused in the doorway.

Now it was Ava's turn to look at her sister in exasperation.

Coach grinned at Alex. "Not *a* film, honey. Just '*film*.' In this case, footage of last year's squad, so I can get a better sense of the strengths and weaknesses of our returners."

Alex pouted. "Oh, right. Never mind." She headed upstairs.

Alone with her mother in the room, Ava moved over to the window again and stared moodily outside.

Mrs. Sackett softly cleared her throat. "Anything wrong, pumpkin?"

Ava shrugged. "Nah. It's just . . . different here. I'll get used to it. I guess I miss my old room. And—my friends and stuff."

"Have you heard from Charlie?" asked her

mother gently, not probing.

Ava nodded and swallowed. "Yeah. I think we're good. I guess he's really excited about football this year—he's been practicing a lot."

Charlie was her best friend back in Massachusetts. Alex was better friends with Charlie's twin, Isabel. Ava and Charlie had been inseparable since T-ball days. Their moms had met at a group for mothers of twins when all the kids were babies, and they had remained good friends. But in the past year, things had been . . . different between her and Charlie. He'd suddenly blushed practically every time she said anything to him. Pass the ketchup, please. Blush. Want to have a catch? Blush. That kind of thing. Well, maybe it was his red hair. Redheaded people blushed easily.

With a heavy sigh, her mom picked up a box marked KITCHEN STUFF. "It's hard for all of us, Ave," she said.

Ava looked at her in surprise. She'd been so busy wallowing in her own self-pity, she hadn't thought about this being hard on her mom. *But*, Ava reflected, *it must be*. Her mom had been really happy back where they used to live. She'd taught art at the local elementary school. She'd had her own friends. A garden.

"Dad is under a lot of pressure as the new coach, and Tommy as a player, too." Ava's mom broke into her thoughts. "At least you and your sister have each other. That's a really special thing."

Ava grimaced. She missed her sister, too. She missed the way they used to hang out together, to take Moxy for walks together, to wash up at the side-by-side sinks in their old bathroom every night. Now they tended to go to bed at different times, and the new bathroom only had one sink. Alex was monopolizing it; she spent what seemed like hours in there with the door closed, experimenting with different hairstyles.

"It seems like we're more different than ever. She's so 'go, go, go!' right now."

"Honey, that's just your sister's way of dealing with all these changes," Mrs. Sackett said. "I know she's been a little . . . intense lately, but she'll be calmer once we've all settled in. You know she feels better when she's working on some sort of project—picking up in Texas where she left off in Boston is her new project."

Ava thought about this. Her mom was right—Alex didn't like change. When she was five, she had thrown a fit when their mom started buying a different brand of peanut butter.

"But you know she needs you to pull her nose out of her planner once in a while," Mrs. Sackett joked.

Ava thought about what her mom said as she climbed into bed. She was just drifting off to sleep when her phone vibrated.

It was Charlie.

Hey, what up? All good in Texas?
You wearing cowboy boots and
a ten-gallon hat yet?

Ha. As if. I'm just trying
not to roast to death.
It was over 100 degrees
again today. ☹

Whoa. You need to find a pool.

Yeah, I think there's one
pretty close to here. We haven't
had time to look for it, though.
How's practice going?

Doesn't start for three weeks.
We're not on the crazy
Texan schedule, remember?
Ha ha.

Oh right. Ha ha.

Ha ha. Well, CU L8ter.

CU L8ter.

Ava read and reread Charlie's texts. Her
first-ever potential crush now lived 1,983 miles
away.

And her twin sister was sleeping a whole
room away. Sigh. Both felt worlds apart.